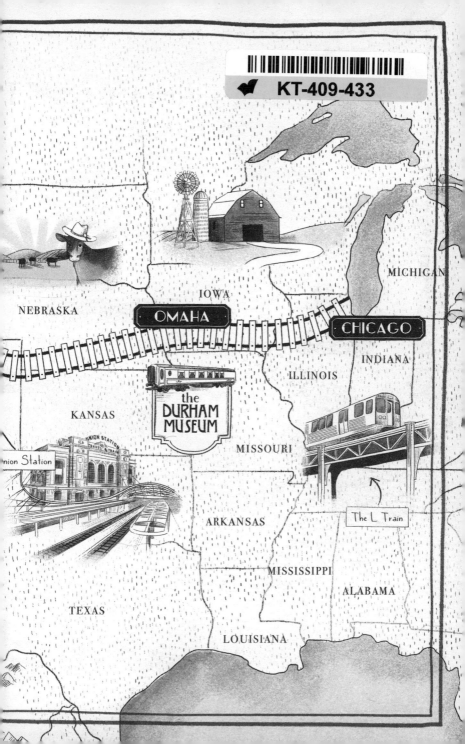

KT-409-433

For my dear friends in America,
Lloydy (aka Dr Simon Jones) and Mike Viola.
I miss you guys.
M. G. Leonard

For my nephew, Monty.
I wish you a lifetime of adventure.
Sam Sedgman

M. G. LEONARD & SAM SEDGMAN

ADVENTURES
ON
TRAINS

KIDNAP ON THE
CALIFORNIA COMET

Illustrated by
Elisa Paganelli

MACMILLAN CHILDREN'S BOOKS

THE CALIFORNIA COMET
ROUTE MAP

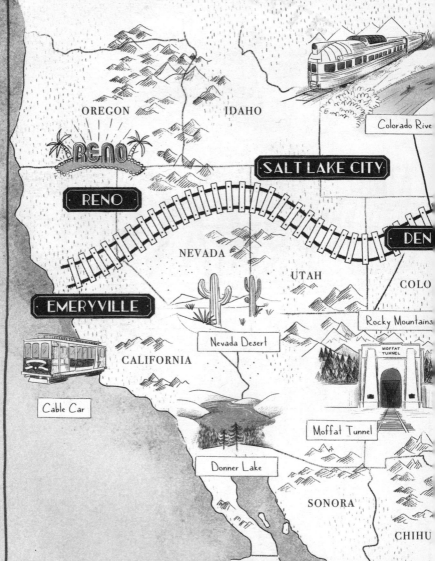

*'Anything is possible on a train: a great meal, a binge,
a visit from card players, an intrigue, a good night's sleep,
and strangers' monologues framed like Russian short stories.'*

Paul Theroux

CHAPTER ONE

CHICAGO

Stepping through the doors of Chicago's Union Station felt like entering a cathedral. Dragging their cases and shaking rain from their coats, Harrison Beck and his uncle Nathaniel Bradshaw stopped to admire the imposing grandeur of the vast marble hall.

'It's like a palace, library and church rolled into one,' said Hal, gazing around.

'A destination station,' Uncle Nat agreed. 'Worthy of a visit even if you're not catching a train. They filmed a famous gangster movie shoot-out here –' he pointed – 'on those steps.'

Hal imagined the white floor splattered with fake blood and shivered.

'Where are the trains?'

'Underground,' said Uncle Nat. 'The tracks snake into the platforms through tunnels beneath the city.'

Hal had spent the previous day riding the 'L' – Chicago's metro system – whose trains clattered between skyscrapers on bridges above the streets, and he laughed. 'The subway is on stilts, and the trains are in tunnels!'

'Exactly!' Uncle Nat said, picking up his suitcase. 'Now come on. Let's find the Metropolitan Lounge.'

Hal followed his uncle down the marble staircase, gripping the brass banister with excitement. He'd been looking forward to this trip for weeks. Life had felt flat and dull after his journey on the Highland Falcon that summer. His baby sister, Ellie, had taken over the house with her bottles, tears and dirty nappies, and his parents were too exhausted to be fun.

But everything had changed when Uncle Nat arrived with Hal's new pet dog, Bailey. The fluffy white Samoyed was fully recovered after the excitement on the royal steam train, and Hal was overjoyed to see her.

'Hal, do you remember me saying I'd been asked to travel across America on the California Comet?' Uncle Nat had said, as Hal rolled around on the floor with Bailey and his mum made tea. 'It just so happens the dates fall in the October school holiday.' His eyes twinkled. 'What do you say? Are you ready for another adventure?'

Hal had whooped, Bailey had barked, and Hal's parents had worried about the cost. But Uncle Nat insisted it would all be taken care of. As a journalist and travel writer, he'd been asked to cover an important press conference being staged by a famous entrepreneur called August Reza. The tickets were being paid for by the newspaper.

'It's your twelfth birthday in October, isn't it?' Uncle Nat said. 'Consider this trip your birthday present.'

Hal had needed to get a passport. He'd also bought a new

sketchbook, a tin of drawing pencils and a sharpener.

The flight to Chicago had been his first time on an aeroplane. The rush of take-off, into a grey English sky, was more alarming than he'd expected. Landing on the other side of the world a few hours later, blinking in the American sunshine, was disorienting. Hal realized he liked to see the places he was travelling through. He was more of a train person than a plane person.

Uncle Nat stopped at the bottom of the station steps, pointing to a distant glass door. 'There's the lounge. I could do with a coffee.'

'I'd like to draw the Great Hall,' said Hal.

'You should. We've plenty of time. Give me your case.' Uncle Nat took the handle. 'Come and find me when you're done. I'll be near the hot drinks.'

Taking out his sketchbook and a pencil, Hal studied the cavernous room. He drew a drum shape in the middle of the page, making the ticket kiosk the focal point of his picture. Vertical lines either side of it became Corinthian columns, holding up the vaulted ceiling, from which hung the stars and stripes of an American flag as large as a ship's sail.

A man in a crumpled suit, carrying a briefcase, paused at the top of the stairs to check his watch. Capturing the figure with the flat side of his pencil, Hal's gaze swept across the white floor. An Amish family had gathered around the ticket kiosk. Their bonnets, hats and aprons made him think of characters from history books. Marking the diagonal lines of the hall's wooden benches, he sketched a red-haired woman

3

in a floor-length blue puffer
coat, sitting with a lizard wrapped around her
shoulders like a scarf. *Is that a bearded dragon?*
Hal wondered as he added her to his picture.

A burly man in a mismatched tracksuit – blue bottoms
and a lime-green top – crossed the concourse, trailed by
a miserable-looking boy in jeans, a red T-shirt, with dental

headgear strapped to his face. The pair passed a muscly man
in a suit and dark glasses, striding purposefully across the hall
with a blonde girl – in a grey pinafore and pink cardigan –
skipping by his side. She smiled at the boy in the headgear and
winked, but he looked away.

As he gazed up at the glass ceiling of the Great Hall, the station bustling around him, the back of Hal's neck prickled, as if he were an antenna picking up a mysterious signal that foretold adventure. He stepped back to take in the hall.

'Hey! Watch it, buddy!'

Spinning around, Hal found himself nose to nose with the bulging blue eyes of a stocky boy with dark hair. 'Sorry! I wasn't looking.' He held up his sketchbook. 'I'm drawing the Great Hall.'

The boy cocked his head. '*I'm drawing the Great Hall*,' he repeated.

Hal frowned, unsure if he was being mocked.

'You're British, aren't you?' the boy asked eagerly. 'Say something else British.'

'I . . . err . . . um . . .'

'*I . . . err . . . um . . .*' the boy imitated, then laughed at the confusion on Hal's face. He swiped his hand. 'Don't mind me. It's a thing I do. You taking a train today?'

Hal nodded. 'I'm taking the California Comet all the way to Emeryville, near San Francisco.'

'Hey, me too!' The boy put his arm around Hal's shoulder. 'This is great. You've gotta meet my sister Hadley. She's in the Metropolitan Lounge. C'mon.'

Hal glanced over his shoulder at the barrel-vaulted skylight. 'But I want to finish—'

'You hungry? I'm starving. The chips and soda in the lounge are free.' The boy patted Hal's back, pushing him towards the glass door. 'Hadley's going to freak when she hears you talk.

6

My name's Mason, by the way. Mason Moretti.'

Surrendering with a shy smile, Hal stuffed his sketchbook and pencil into the pocket of his yellow anorak. 'I'm Harrison Beck, but everybody calls me Hal.'

'This way, Hal.' Mason guided him into the lounge towards a table where a girl with wavy honey-coloured hair was playing cards. 'Hey, Hadley! Meet Hal.'

Hadley looked round, sweeping up her deck of cards in one impressively fluid movement. She was wearing a purple hoodie with white writing on the front: *What the eyes see, and the ears hear, the mind believes – Harry Houdini.*

'Hi.' She smiled at Hal. Her teeth were perfect.

'Hal's British.' Mason nudged him. 'Go on, say something.'

'Pleased to meet you,' Hal said, feeling himself blush.

'*Pleased to meet you,*' Mason mimicked.

'I wish you wouldn't do that,' Hal mumbled.

'*I wish you wouldn't do that,*' Mason repeated.

'Mason copies everyone.' Hadley's brown eyes were warm, and her manner friendly. 'It's infuriating, but his impressions are really good.'

'I've never had a Brit to impersonate before.' Mason looked at Hal like a hungry dog looks at a steak. 'I know – say the alphabet for me! Wait, I need my recorder. You gotta be in my voice bank.'

'Voice bank?'

'I collect voices so I can practise the sounds and shapes of words.' Mason stretched and squashed his mouth into several alarming positions, making vowel sounds. His olive

7

skin was remarkably elastic.

'You don't want my voice,' Hal said. 'I'm northern, from a place called Crewe. I'm not posh like the Queen.' He didn't like the idea of spending his train journey being a guinea pig for an impressionist's voice bank.

'How old are you?' Hadley asked.

'Twelve,' Hal replied, not admitting it had only been three days since his birthday.

'Me too.'

'I'm thirteen,' said Mason.

'Really?'

Hadley giggled. 'Everyone thinks Mason's my *little* brother.'

'There's nothing wrong with being short,' Mason snapped. 'All the best actors are short, and I haven't finished growing.'

Hal sensed this was the beginning of an often-repeated quarrel and changed the subject. 'Didn't you say there were free chips?'

'Yeah, over here.' Mason took him to a counter and a bowl of brightly coloured crisp packets.

'They're not chips.'

'Yes they are,' Mason said.

'Chips are potatoes.'

'Exactly.'

'Chips are hot, and you dip them in ketchup. These are crisps.'

'He means fries,' Hadley said, grabbing a packet and pulling it open.

'You call fries *chips*, and chips *crisps*?' Mason shook his head. 'Wild.'

'America's confusing,' Hal said, taking a bag of crisps. 'Yesterday I ordered a pizza, but when it came, it was a pie!'

'Mmm, deep-dish pizza.' Hadley smacked her lips. 'That's a Chicago specialty.'

'*There* you are, Hal.' Uncle Nat appeared at the foot of the staircase. He stood out from the crowd in his rainbow-striped sweater, petrol-blue suit and spotless white trainers. 'Already making friends?'

'This is Mason and Hadley,' Hal said, introducing them.

'A pleasure to meet you.' Uncle Nat shook their hands. 'I'm Hal's uncle, Nathaniel Bradshaw.'

Hal saw Mason silently mouth, '*A pleasure to meet you.*'

'Are you taking the California Comet?' Uncle Nat asked.

'Yeah. We're going to Reno,' Hadley replied, trying to divert Uncle Nat's attention away from Mason. 'Pop's working at a casino there.'

'Is your father a croupier?'

'He's an entertainer,' Hadley said.

'How fascinating.'

'*How fascinating,*' Mason echoed quietly.

'Hal, it's time to check our bags into the luggage car,' Uncle Nat said. He nodded at Hadley and Mason. 'I'm sure we'll meet again on the train.'

Waving goodbye, Hal pulled on his rucksack and helped his uncle drag their suitcases out of the lounge. A busker with a saxophone had set up in the hall, and Uncle Nat drifted over, enjoying the music. Hal whipped out his sketchbook. He only needed a few moments more to finish his drawing. When the song ended, Uncle Nat dropped a couple of dollar bills into the musician's case, and he and Hal walked together to the luggage desk. As he followed his uncle across the concourse, Hal wished he were more like him. Uncle Nat seemed at home wherever he was.

After securing their suitcases with small padlocks, and checking them in, Uncle Nat paused in front of a large map of the United States, placing the keys in his jacket pocket, and pulling out their tickets.

'We want the south gate, track F. The California Comet is train five.'

'What's Amtrak?' Hal asked, pointing at the map, which had *The Amtrak System* written above it. Red lines criss-crossed the country, marking the railway routes.

'Amtrak run the passenger trains in America.' Uncle Nat pointed at a dot in the middle of the map, below a big lake. 'We're here, in Chicago.' His finger traced a red line west. 'We'll travel through the farmlands of Iowa and Nebraska, up through the snow-capped Rocky Mountains in Colorado, cross the desert in Utah, and make passage through the forests of the Sierra Nevada. From there we'll sweep south-west to the California coast, arriving in San Francisco in two days' time.'

Hal looked up at his uncle and they shared a grin – like skydivers ready to leap. 'Let's go and find our train,' he said.

CHAPTER TWO

THE SILVER SCOUT

Descending a sloping walkway, they came to a row of underground platforms, each beside a train as tall as Hal's house.

'They're huge!' Hal exclaimed.

'Double-deckers,' said Uncle Nat, walking towards track F. 'Quite standard in Europe. It's us Brits who have small trains.'

'Why?'

'Our bridges and tunnels are low. You'd never fit one of these Superliners through Box Tunnel.' Uncle Nat came to a halt and let out a low whistle. 'Well, would you look at that?'

He was staring at an old silver bullet-shaped train carriage, polished so it looked brand new. An art deco sign above a row of tinted windows read *CALIFORNIA COMET*, and a smaller sign beneath them read *SILVER SCOUT*.

Hal gaped at it. It was beautiful.

'That is one of the original six Vista Dome observation cars built for the California Comet in 1948.' Uncle Nat spoke in a hushed voice as they approached it. 'I'd heard August Reza had refurbished one as his private railcar.' He looked at Hal. 'This must be it.'

'*Private* railcar?' Hal had never heard of such a thing.

'Your own carriage, to attach to any train.' Uncle Nat shook his head. 'I wonder what it's like inside?' He reverently brushed his fingertips over the *SILVER SCOUT* sign.

Hal slid off his rucksack, kneeling on it as he tugged his sketchbook from his pocket. 'I'm going to draw it.' He pulled out his tin of pencils and sharpened one to a fine point. Leaning the book on his knees, he drew a squared-off bullet shape and the corrugated grooves that marked the body of the carriage. He outlined the edge of the neon light in the bottom panel of the rear door that blazed *CALIFORNIA COMET* in red.

'I'm going to have a peek around the other side,' said Uncle Nat, disappearing.

Hal sketched the domed roof. The curved window panels in silver frames that rose up from the centre of the carriage reminded him of an aircraft gunner turret.

'What do you think you're doing, kid?'

Hal froze. It was the muscly man from the Great Hall. 'I'm drawing the Silver Scout, sir.' He held up his sketchbook.

The man folded his arms, his biceps bulging. 'That's a *private* carriage.'

'Leave him alone, Woody.' The blonde girl in the pink cardigan Hal had seen earlier stepped out from behind him. She looked older than Hal, but not by much. She glanced at his drawing and smiled. 'Hey, that's good!' There was a touch of French to her soft American accent. 'I draw too – comics mainly. I copy *Asterix* and *Tintin* to practise, but I also make up my own.'

'It's just an outline,' Hal said, getting to his feet. 'I'll work

14

on it later, on the train. Isn't it the coolest carriage you've ever seen?'

'It's my father's.' The girl shrugged, apparently unimpressed.

'Oh!' *This must be August Reza's daughter!* Hal thought. Remembering Uncle Nat's job to cover the press conference, he held out his hand politely. 'My name's Harrison.'

Woody stuck out an arm to prevent the handshake, but the girl side-stepped, grabbing Hal's hand with both of hers.

'Miss Reza!'

'Oh, calm down, Woody.' She tutted. 'He's hardly going to attack me with you standing there like a great ogre. Or are you worried he'd beat you in a fight?'

Hal dared not smile in case he angered the man, who he realized must be her bodyguard.

'I'm Marianne. Are you coming on the California Comet?'

'Yes – I'm going to San Francisco with my uncle. How far are you travelling?'

'*Pfff.*' She blew out a sulky breath that kicked up her fringe. 'Who knows? I do what my father decides. I'm told nothing. But we live in Silicon Valley, which is not far from there.'

'Oh, I see,' said Hal. Marianne clearly wasn't happy about going on this train journey. He remembered how he'd first felt about being shipped off on the Highland Falcon. 'Maybe it won't be so bad.'

Woody cleared his throat loudly.

'Bah, *oui!*' Marianne snapped, rolling her eyes at Woody. 'I must go. Maybe I will see you on the train.' She leaned forward, kissing the air in front of his cheeks. On the second

15

kiss, she whispered, 'I'll escape the ogre and come find you. Perhaps we can draw?' She stepped back, waved her fingertips, and allowed Woody to shepherd her into the Silver Scout.

Dumbfounded, Hal stared at the carriage door. It was the most baffling encounter he'd ever had with a girl. He wished his friend Lenny were with him. She'd be able to explain what had just happened.

'Have you finished your drawing?' Uncle Nat was striding towards him. 'We should find our carriage.'

Hal nodded and followed his uncle along the platform. The double-decker carriages were the same silver as the Rezas' railcar but dented and scuffed. Between the windows of the top and bottom floors was a blue band, topped by a thin red-and-white stripe.

'This is us.' Uncle Nat pointed. 'Carriage 540.'

Stepping inside, they were met by a woman in a dark-blue uniform with curly brown hair. 'Y'all travelling with us today?'

'Indeed we are,' Uncle Nat replied.

'Well, good! Your tickets, please, sir.' The woman beamed as she examined them. 'You're in the right place. I'm Francine, your steward. You gentlemen are in roomette ten. I'll show you up.' She led them past a luggage rack and up a slender flight of stairs.

'We're on the top floor!' Hal exclaimed.

'Sure are.' Francine smiled at him over her shoulder.

On either side of the upper corridor were sliding doors through which Hal could see tiny compartments, each containing two big blue seats facing one another.

'You'll be right here.' Francine stood aside to let them in. 'Get yourselves comfortable, and I'll be back to see about your dinner reservations. Anything you need, call out my name.'

'Home, sweet home.' Uncle Nat sighed happily. He slid the door shut and dropped his leather holdall on to one of the big blue seats.

Hal clambered on to the other one, pulling at handles and flicking switches, eager to discover the secrets of the roomette. It was snug, but the seats were wide and they had enough room. 'This is cool.' A table marked with a chessboard folded out from beneath the window. 'Do you think Francine has pieces?'

'Probably.' Uncle Nat pointed to the plug socket. 'Look! You'll be able to charge your games console.'

'I didn't bring it.'

'Really?' Uncle Nat looked surprised.

'I didn't want to miss anything.' Hal felt his face grow hot. 'If I'm gaming, I might not notice an adventure, you know, if one happens.'

'I am glad,' Uncle Nat said. 'Though it's unlikely we'll encounter another adventure quite like the last one.'

'It doesn't hurt to be alert though, does it?' Hal thought about Marianne Reza and her muscle-bound bodyguard, wondering if she would escape and come looking for him.

'No,' Uncle Nat said, taking off his glasses, cleaning them with the bottom of his jumper and putting them back on. 'And an adventure doesn't always have to involve a crime.'

'The exciting ones do.'

Uncle Nat laughed. 'You'll end up being a railway detective when you grow up.'

Hal thought that wouldn't be a bad job. He pointed to a panel above the window. 'If the top bunk is up there, where's the other one?'

'You're sitting on it.' Uncle Nat fiddled with a catch near the floor and, with a jolt, Hal's chair slid forward, becoming flat as it met the opposite seat. 'Nice!'

Uncle Nat sat down beside

Hal. 'Through that window you'll get to see the wonders of America. It's an incredible place.'

'I thought it would be like England, but it isn't, is it? Everything is *extra*, here. The roads are wider; the cars are bigger; even the food portions are huge.' Hal paused, momentarily overcome by the scale of America. 'It makes me feel small.'

'You'll get used to it. And then when you go home, you'll think everything in Crewe is tiny.' Uncle Nat looked at him over his glasses. 'Travelling changes you. Marvelling at new places is an important part of that. It makes you think about different ways of living.'

He pulled his journal and pencil case from his bag

and placed it in a nook beside the chair. 'This can be my seat.' Pulling back his sleeve, he looked at one of the three watches on his left wrist. At first, Hal had thought it odd that his uncle wore six watches – they told the time in London, New York, Tokyo, Berlin, Sydney and Moscow – but each was a souvenir from his travels, and Uncle Nat had explained that he liked to be aware of the rest of the world, wherever he was. 'We've just enough time to stroll up the platform and see the locomotive, if you'd like?'

'Let's do it.' Hal jumped to his feet and opened the door. He found himself staring at a woman with shiny lips and thick caramel-coloured hair pulled up into a topknot. She was wearing a black leather jacket, grey sweater and jeans. She glared at him. 'Oh! Hello.'

'You must be our neighbour,' Uncle Nat said, smiling. 'I'm Nathaniel Bradshaw, and this is Harrison.'

'Vanessa Rodriguez,' she replied, dropping her heavy bag into the roomette opposite with a *thunk*! Stepping in, she slid the door shut and drew the blue curtain across the window.

'I'm guessing she doesn't want to be disturbed,' Uncle Nat whispered. 'Let's go.'

Jumping down the stairs and jogging along the platform, they passed the single-storey baggage car, where cases were being loaded from a forklift truck. As they approached the front of the train, the rumble of engines grew to a roar that made Hal's ribs vibrate. The air stank of diesel.

Two blue-and-silver locomotives growled in the shadows of the underground station, their vents thrumming with exhaust. Each was the size of an articulated lorry and had a face – a pair of shadow-filled windscreens above two blazing pairs of circular headlights.

'They're not as friendly-looking as steam engines!' Hal had to shout so Uncle Nat could hear him above the noise.

'Diesel-electric,' Uncle Nat called back, nodding. 'Genesis class. There's a power plant in her belly with twice as much horsepower as an A4 Pacific.' He gazed at the engines. 'Magnificent!'

21

'Why are there two?'

'They have to drag this very heavy train up the Rocky Mountains.' Uncle Nat waved at the carriages. 'If there were only one engine, and it failed, we'd be in trouble.'

Hal stared at the leading locomotive. It glowered back at him. He slipped his hand into his pocket and realized his sketchbook was back in the roomette, so he studied the engine's shapes, hoping to draw it from memory.

Uncle Nat touched Hal's arm and pointed. The luggage car doors were being shut and empty baggage trailers driven away. 'Time to go.'

Walking back, Hal saw Francine leaning out the door, flapping her hands at them to hurry. They broke into a run, and she laughed as they scrambled aboard. 'I wouldn't have let them leave without you!' she said, as the carriage door shut behind them.

Tumbling into their roomette, Hal and Nat dropped into their seats just as the concrete pillars of Union Station slid past the window.

'What's this?' Uncle Nat leaned down, picking up an envelope from the floor. He pulled out a card and drew in a delighted breath. 'Hal! It's a message from August Reza. We've been invited to visit him in the Silver Scout!'

CHAPTER THREE

REZA'S EDGE

Daylight flooded the roomette as the California Comet pulled out of the station. The window scene of Chicago skyscrapers became concrete highways, then widely spaced houses, then stunning autumn trees with leaves of burnished gold and fading magenta.

'It's an hour from Naperville to Princeton,' Uncle Nat said gleefully, slipping a notepad and pen into his jacket pocket. 'Plenty of time to explore the railcar – and quiz August Reza before tonight's press conference.'

'Can't we go now?' Hal was eager to see the inside of the Silver Scout and wondered if Marianne would be there.

'There's no connecting door.' Uncle Nat shook his head. 'Reza's railcar is much older than the Superliners. You can only get into the Silver Scout from a station platform – that's why we have to wait for the train to stop.'

'So once we board in Naperville, we won't be able to leave until we reach Princeton?'

'Precisely.' Uncle Nat looked out the window, his eyes following the track. 'I'm dying to know what tonight's press conference is about. I wonder if he'll drop any hints.'

'What does August Reza do?'

'He's a technology entrepreneur. He made his fortune developing batteries.'

'Batteries?' Hal was surprised to hear you could make a fortune out of something as ordinary as a battery.

'Not the kind of battery you buy in a supermarket. Special batteries – the kind that power satellites or deep-sea drilling equipment.' Uncle Nat looked at Hal. 'He invested in electric cars, robotics, AI, phones . . . All powered by his batteries, of course. If you think about it, every electronic device depends on a battery.'

'Is the press conference going to be about batteries?' Hal pulled a face at the thought of having to sit through something that boring, and Uncle Nat laughed.

'Nobody knows. It's a secret, which, of course, is making everyone excited.'

'Maybe it's about trains,' Hal said, 'and that's why you've been invited – because you're an expert.'

'Perhaps.' Uncle Nat shrugged. 'To be honest, I don't know. I'm sure I'm not the only journalist on this train. Look, we're slowing down. Let's go.'

The California Comet pulled alongside a red brick building with a blue sign announcing it was Naperville station. The train door wheezed opened, and they sprang out on to the platform, hurrying to the Silver Scout. Uncle Nat rapped on the door. It was opened by Marianne's bodyguard, who looked down at them with a blank expression.

'Hi, Woody,' Hal said cheerfully. 'This is my uncle, Nathaniel Bradshaw. Mr Reza invited us to visit.'

Uncle Nat stared at Hal in surprise. Hal nudged him. 'Oh, um, yes.' He held up the invitation. 'We're invited.'

Woody grunted and beckoned them in.

'How do you know him?' Uncle Nat whispered as they followed Woody down a serene white polycarbonate corridor.

'I'll tell you later,' Hal replied, enjoying his uncle's astonishment.

They passed four white doors with handles of brushed aluminium. One opened a crack, and Hal thought he glimpsed Marianne.

Two steps down, and Hal found himself in a futuristic room the full width of the carriage. In the middle, an ebony oval table stood perched on one central silver leg. Beyond it, reclining on a carbon-fibre sofa, was an elegant woman with luminous umber skin, dressed in a red pantsuit and zebra-print stilettos. Standing opposite her was a bald man in a dark turtleneck jumper and clear-frame glasses. The woman's ruby-red lips parted. She had a dazzling smile. 'Nat Bradshaw, it's been a long time,' she said, getting to her feet.

'Zola.' Uncle Nat bowed his head. 'I should have guessed you'd be here.'

'Nat,' Zola said, 'allow me to introduce you to my *good friend* August Reza.'

'A pleasure to meet you, sir.' Uncle Nat shook August Reza's hand.

'I've read more than a couple of your books,' August replied. 'The pleasure is mine.' He turned to Hal. 'And you must be Harrison.'

Hal, finding himself tongue-tied, nodded as August shook his hand.

'Hal,' Uncle Nat said, 'this is Zola D'Ormond, she's a . . . colleague of mine.'

'Rival, more like.' Zola winked at Hal. 'I'm a journalist too.'

'Let's have a drink,' said August. 'Woody, bring us some juice.'

'Could I get a gingerberry sparkler?' Zola purred.

'I was delighted to get your invitation,' said Uncle Nat, his face boyishly excited. 'I never dreamed I'd get to travel in an original Vista Dome.'

'Isn't she something?' August waved his hand. 'I designed the interior myself. Would you like to see it?'

Hal and Uncle Nat both nodded enthusiastically. 'Yes, please,' they said in unison.

'On the way in, you passed a restroom, the staff cabin – where Woody and my chef sleep – the galley, and my daughter's compartment.'

It *was* Marianne that Hal had spied through the gap in the door.

'This is my meeting room. We'll be holding the second half of the press conference in here this evening.'

'How will you fit everybody in?' Zola asked, looking around.

'Table – *down*.' Reza said, and responding to his voice, the silver leg retracted into itself like an antenna.

'Cool!' Hal whispered as he watched it sink into an opening that appeared in the floor.

'The sofas –' August walked to the far end of the room – 'will be moved into here.' He led them up a couple of steps into the rounded tail of the carriage, where a panoramic window stretched around the room. 'This is my viewing lounge.'

Hal was momentarily hypnotized by the endless unreeling track, but then August Reza rapped his knuckles on the window.

'Bulletproof, of course.' He paused, and Hal could tell he was enjoying their expressions of awe as they took in the built-in cocktail bar and the view. 'Shall we go upstairs?'

'There's an upstairs?' Hal asked.

August put his foot on the bottom step of a clear Perspex staircase and smiled. 'Come see.'

Hal eagerly climbed into the room with the Vista Dome ceiling. August stood at the foot of a low Japanese-style double bed of black bamboo topped with white linen.

'This is my bedroom.' August pointed to the corner, past a white desk with two thin monitors and a keyboard. 'Down those stairs is the ensuite.'

'Budge up,' Uncle Nat said, climbing the stairs behind Hal.

Hal went to sit on the small sofa opposite the desk to make room and looked up at the cloudy sky through the domed roof. 'This carriage is amazing.'

Uncle Nat sat beside him. 'Isn't it just?'

'Doesn't the light bother you, in the morning?' Zola propped herself against the desk, brushing against the

27

computer mouse. The screens lit up. 'Oops.'

August stepped over to the computer and shut it down. 'I have voice-activated blackout blinds,' he said, giving her a pointed look.

'Of course.' Zola looked down.

'Hal –' August wheeled around – 'if you like trains as much as your uncle, I've got something you should see.' He beckoned for them to follow him back downstairs.

'Nice move, bringing a kid.' Zola said under her breath to Uncle Nat. 'Everyone knows Reza's a sucker for children.'

Uncle Nat didn't reply, and Hal wondered what Zola meant.

In the conference room, the black oval table was rising back up.

'Table – *open*,' Reza commanded, and the surface split in two.

Hal's eyes grew wide. Inside the table was a perfectly scaled model city, rising up as the table-top folded under. Between the miniature skyscrapers and manicured parks, a sleek silver train with an aerodynamic nose, like a rocket cone, whizzed around an elevated railway track. On the side of the locomotive, engraved under the word *Mari,* was the number 70707.

Woody arrived with a tray of green drinks and one fizzing pink, floating with cranberries, ice and a black stick. He picked up a silver pistol from the tray, a flame springing from its end and lit the sparkler, before handing the drink to Zola.

'Toy trains – how adorable,' Zola said, sounding bored. 'Come and look at the view with me, Nat.' She snaked her hand through his arm as he picked up his green juice and pulled him back up the steps into the viewing lounge.

Hal saw his uncle cast a wistful glance over his shoulder at the model railway as he left.

'This is brilliant!' Hal leaned down to study every detail of the miniature city. 'Did you make it?'

'Yes.' August Reza bent down, his face beside Hal's. 'It's my vision of the future. A world where transport is clean and affordable for everyone, where fossil fuels are obsolete, and carbon stays in the ground. The key is a new type of train. A new train is our best chance of an affordable mode of mass transport that reduces carbon emissions.'

'Dad's not going on about his *visions,* is he?' Marianne said from the doorway.

'Hal this is Marianne, my daughter.'

'We've met.' Marianne took a glass of the green juice

from Woody's tray and sucked on the aluminium straw.

'Mari, you know, all of this is for you.' August Reza went over to stand beside his daughter, stroking her hair. 'Who d'you think will inherit this planet after my generation is gone?'

'Urgh, Dad. So morbid!'

Woody offered Hal a drink.

'What is it?' He took one and sniffed it. 'It smells like grass.'

'Green juice,' said Marianne. 'It's all anyone drinks in California.'

Hal took a sip and immediately spat it back into the glass. 'Urgh, it tastes like compost!'

Marianne giggled, putting her empty glass back on the tray. 'You get used to it.'

'Mari, why don't you and Hal go play?' August Reza smiled indulgently.

Marianne looked at Hal, then nodded. 'C'mon,' she said to him.

'*Go play!*' she scoffed once they were in the corridor. 'Pop thinks I'm still six.'

'He's nice.' Hal followed her into her compartment.

'Yeah, when he's not having one of his *visions*.' She scowled. 'He says I'm the most important thing in his life, but he sends me away to boarding school for most of the year in France. If I was

31

that important, he'd spend the school holidays doing father-and-daughter stuff. But no – he brings me on this dumb train while he works on his *vision* and ignores me.'

Hal wasn't sure what to say. 'I'm sorry.'

'Don't be.' Marianne slid her cabin door shut behind them. 'Mom's just as bad. She works for the UN – always flying around trying to save people. I don't need saving, so she pretty much ignores me too.' She sighed. 'When they were married, we'd do family things – like holidays and outings, but since they split up . . .' She sat down heavily on her bunk.

The compartment would have seemed clinical if it weren't for Marianne's belongings. Her duvet was pink and dotted with dancing flamingos. On it rested a wooden drawing board with a neat pile of paper, a ruler lined up beside it, and a fine-point pen. Her shelves held comic books ordered by height. Beneath them, on a slim desk, a collection of pens and pencils were divided neatly by colour into glass jars: tomato red, grass green, midnight blue . . . A rainbow stretching all the way to fuchsia. 'You have a jar for every colour?'

'Yeah.' Marianne shrugged, pulling the drawing board towards her. 'I wanted to show you this.'

The page she held up was divided into panels. In the top-left panel was the outline of a boy kneeling in front of a silver train carriage, drawing.

'Is that me?'

'I'm not as good at drawing as you,' Marianne said, suddenly self-conscious. 'But I like making stories with pictures and words, writing adventures.'

'Am I going to be in your adventure?'

'Guess you are.' Marianne smiled. 'Do you want some candy?' From her pocket, she pulled a couple of sweets wrapped in purple foil and handed him one. Unwrapping hers, she popped it in her mouth. 'Mmmm, blackcurrant liquorice – my favourite.'

Hal hated liquorice. He read *Cassis Réglisse Noire* in tiny black swirling letters on the sweet. 'I'll have mine later.' He said, putting it in his pocket and pulling out his sketchbook. 'When I draw, I try to capture moments.' He opened it to his picture of Union Station and pointed.

Marianne squinted. 'Is that me?'

'A tiny you.' Hal nodded. 'I'm going to draw the inside of the Silver Scout when I get back to the roomette.'

'You can do it now.' Marianne indicated for him to sit on the end of her bed. 'It's ages till the next station. I'll do my story too.'

Hal sat cross-legged on the bunk beside her and leaned his sketchbook on his knees. He pulled out his pencil and began to draw the conference room with its hidden model railway. Looking over at the pots of pens, he spotted a silver one and reached out to grab it. But as the train rocked, his hand slipped, knocking into the jars and sending red, green and blue pens tumbling to the floor.

'*No!*' Marianne screeched, leaping to her feet. 'You idiot!'

'Sorry.' Hal scrambled down, picking up the pens. 'It was an accident. . . *Ow!*'

Marianne had grabbed him by his hair and was pulling

him up. 'Don't touch them!' she snapped. 'You'll do it wrong.'

'You're hurting me.' Hal put his hand to hers, and she let go of his hair. He gaped at her, shocked by her sudden outburst, and stepped back.

There was a knock at the door.

'We're approaching Princeton,' Uncle Nat called out.

'Coming!' Hal shoved the pens he'd collected off the floor at Marianne. She took them and, turning her back, began sorting them into piles on her bed.

Uncle Nat and Zola were by the carriage door. Hal joined them as the train came to a stand-still, feeling shaken by Marianne's outburst. The three of them stepped down on to a grassy trackside verge. Uncle Nat gave Zola his arm as she picked her way in her high heels to the short platform.

'That is the most impressive railcar I've seen in my life,' Uncle Nat said.

'Even better than the Highland Falcon?' Hal asked, rubbing the sore patch on the top of his head.

'Pullmans are exquisite, but the Silver Scout is out of this world.'

'What did August's daughter talk to you about?' Zola asked Hal with interest.

'We talked about drawing.' Hal frowned, thinking about the things Marianne had said about her dad.

'Did she mention what August's plans were for the press conference this evening?'

'No.' Hal couldn't shake the image of Marianne glaring at him. 'But when you two were in the viewing lounge, Mr Reza said something about a new train. *A train of the future.*'

Zola and Uncle Nat stopped walking and stared at him.

'That *is* interesting.' Zola let go of Uncle Nat's arm and stepped up beside Hal. 'Look, the next carriage is mine, but wouldn't it be fun if we dined together tonight, before the press conference?' She smiled at him. 'Wouldn't that be fun?'

'All three of us?' Uncle Nat asked, sounding amused.

'Oh, yes.' Zola smiled. 'All three of us.'

CHAPTER FOUR

A SECRET MESSAGE

'I'm confused. Is Zola your friend?' Hal climbed into his seat in the roomette, sitting cross-legged. His head was sore, and he wondered whether he should tell Uncle Nat about Marianne's outburst.

'Zola and I are journalists,' Uncle Nat replied. 'We've known each other a long time, and we've covered some of the same stories over the years. She's excellent at her job. Fiercely protective of her sources and always manages to be one step ahead of . . . well, everybody. The last time I saw her, she was angry with me. I'd done an exclusive interview with a businessman in the rail industry – and accidentally broke a story she'd been working on about a corporate takeover.' His nose twitched and there was a hint of a smile in his eyes. 'I don't think she's forgiven me.' He paused. 'Yes. Dinner is going to be interesting. Try to avoid telling her too much.'

'About what?'

'Anything she wants to know about.' Uncle Nat replied.

Hal nodded, looking out at the flat farmland zipping

past the window. He remembered Zola saying Uncle Nat had brought Hal on the Comet to get close to August Reza and wondered if it was true. *No*, Hal thought. He and Uncle Nat were friends. They shared a love of trains. No other adult treated Hal with the respect his uncle did – not even his parents. He thought of his family and was suddenly aware of how far away they were. *Mum and Dad, Ellie and Bailey – they're on the other side of the world*, he thought, feeling a ripple of nausea ruffling his insides. *I miss them. I miss home.*

Francine's warm sing-song voice came through a speaker in the corridor announcing the dining car was open for lunch.

'You hungry yet?' Uncle Nat asked.

'I don't know,' Hal replied. 'I feel a bit mixed up.'

'Food might be just what you need to sort you out. Come on – let's see what's on the menu.'

The dining car was in the middle of the train. Using the corridor that snaked between carriages on the upper floor, they passed through two sleeping cars before reaching the end of the queue of people waiting to be seated for lunch. Hal looked into the bustling restaurant. It was like the American diners he'd seen in movies: blue vinyl booths, each with a silver-rimmed Formica table.

'Please wait to be seated,' said a waiter in a navy apron and blue tie. 'We're carrying hot food and drinks, and we don't want you to be wearing that food.' He gave them a broad smile and his bald head wrinkled. 'My name is Earl. I'll be seating you four to a table. If you come for lunch with a party of three or fewer, you'll be seated with a brand-new friend.

37

Why not use this opportunity to get to know someone on Amtrak?'

Hal saw Vanessa Rodriguez, their sullen roomette neighbour, was at the front of the line.

'Party of one, Miss?' Earl asked.

'Mm-huh.' Vanessa nodded, then jerked her head and slapped her hand against the wall, making a loud bang.

Earl jumped, and everyone in the queue stiffened.

Vanessa sniffed, glancing down at the floor, before following him to a table.

'Let's hope we don't get sat with her,' Uncle Nat said under his breath. 'Not sure she wants to get to know anyone on Amtrak.'

'Party of two?' the waiter asked the man and boy ahead of Hal and Nat. They nodded. 'Party of two?' he asked Uncle Nat, who also nodded. 'Neat. Follow me, please.'

As Hal passed the spot Vanessa had looked at, he noticed a dead fly lying on the floor, and realized she'd swatted it.

Sitting down at the table, Hal saw that a workstation of hatches and drawers divided the room. Earl took three steaming plates of food out of a hatch and delivered them to another table. Hal could hear the sound of crashing pots and sizzling meat coming from downstairs.

Looking at their lunch companions, Hal saw he was sitting opposite the boy in dental headgear that he'd sketched in Union Station. He tried not to stare, but the blue bands that covered the boy's forehead and cupped his chin looked uncomfortable. Metal rods, attached to each side of the plastic stood proud of the boy's cheeks. Tiny screws attached the face scaffolding to the braces on his top and bottom teeth. A broad black elastic strap crossed over the boy's cropped hair, holding the contraption in place. Tucked into the sides, over his ears, were big red thick-lensed glasses.

'Hello.' Hal smiled warmly. 'My name's Harrison.'

'Harro Harriron,' the boy replied quietly, looking down at the table. 'My name ee Ryron.'

'*Ryron?*' Hal leaned forward, trying to catch the boy's eyes to make sure he'd heard him correctly. Americans had unusual names.

The athletic man in the mismatching tracksuit sat beside him, laughed, and clapped an enormous hand on the unfortunate boy's back, almost knocking the glasses off his face. 'My son's name is Ryan. He can't speak great on account of all that metal strapped to his teeth.' The man reached his hand over the table to shake Uncle Nat's. 'I'm Gene. Gene Jackson. I coach gym. Wrestling's my sport. You like sport?'

'I do.' Uncle Nat shook his hand, and Hal noticed him wince as Gene crushed it. 'Nathaniel Bradshaw. My nephew Hal and I landed yesterday morning, but we managed to fit in a basketball game at the United Center in Chicago last night – Bulls versus the Pistons.'

'Basketball? How about that!' Gene Jackson leered at Hal. 'Did you dig it?'

Hal nodded. 'It was fast and loud, and I don't think I understood the rules completely, but . . .'

'I thought, being as you're British, you'd be into cricket

and teapots.' Gene stroked his chin and looked at Uncle Nat. 'Who's your team?'

'I don't really have a team. I find sport is an excellent way to get to know a place and understand how its people—'

'I'm here for the LA Lakers,' Gene interrupted, patting his chest. 'I like winners.'

Hal noticed a silver sports whistle hanging on a yellow ribbon around Gene's neck. His own hand went instinctively to the precious train whistle hidden beneath his jumper. It was engraved with the name of the Highland Falcon. Lenny – his best friend – had posted it to him when he'd called to tell her he was going to America to travel on the California Comet. They shared the whistle. It was her turn to have it, but she'd insisted he take it for the journey.

'Gentlemen –' Earl handed them menus – 'can I get you something to drink?'

'I'll have a Dr Pepper,' Gene replied. 'You want a Dr Pepper, Ryan?' Ryan shook his head. 'Yeah, make that two Dr Peppers.'

'I'll have still water, please,' Uncle Nat said.

'Me too.' Hal looked at the menu, scanning soups, salads, pastas, and lingering over the list of burgers. He realized he was hungry. He wondered if Mason and Hadley would be coming to the diner for lunch. He didn't like the idea of being Mason's vocal dummy, but at least Mason wouldn't pull his hair.

Earl disappeared and arrived back a few moments later. 'Here you go.' He placed the drinks on the table. 'You ready to order?'

'Hal?' Uncle Nat asked.

'The Angus burger and fries looks good.'

'Strong choice, young man,' Earl said, writing his order down.

'Same for Ryan,' Gene said, 'and I'll have the baked chilaquiles, with a side of fries.'

'I'd like the steamed mussels and garden salad,' Uncle Nat said.

'You'd better sit back while Ryan's eating,' Gene said. 'It can get messy, if you know what I mean?' He laughed loudly and Ryan's neck flushed pink.

Hal felt a flash of sympathy for Ryan. Marianne might be angry with her father for being obsessed with his work, but at least August Reza was nice.

'Are you travelling to San Francisco?' Uncle Nat asked Gene, changing the subject to move the focus from Ryan.

'Yup – I'm taking my boy to a wrestling tournament.' He ran his fingers through his greased-back hair. 'Gonna show him how the champs do it.'

Ryan looked downcast. Hal tried and failed to catch his eye. Uncle Nat and Gene fell into a conversation about the rules of wrestling, so he took his sketchbook out and opened it to a clean page. 'I like to draw,' he said quietly to Ryan. 'Do you draw?'

Ryan shook his head.

Pulling out a pencil, Hal speedily drew his view down the dining car. Practice had made him confident and quick with his lines.

'So, you're tourists,' Gene said.

'I like to think we are travellers, but I'm also doing a bit of work while we're here.'

'What work?'

'I'm a journalist. I'm attending a press conference in Omaha.'

'Do you know August Reza?'

Hal frowned, thinking that if a man like Gene Jackson had heard about the press conference, August Reza must be very famous.

'Not especially,' Uncle Nat replied. 'We met for the first time this morning.'

'We went in Mr Reza's private carriage,' Hal said to Ryan. 'It's really cool. It old on the outside, but inside it's ultra-modern – like a spaceship.'

Ryan leaned forward, watching as Hal sketched the man at the opposite table – napkin tucked in his shirt collar, a briefcase beside his leg.

He gave Hal a timid smile and held his hand out for the pencil.

'You want a go?' Hal flipped over to a clean page and pushed the pad and pencil towards him.

But Ryan turned the page back to Hal's drawing. Hal watched,

confused, as Ryan chose some of his lines to go over. He pushed the graphite tip hard into the paper, almost tearing it. It took every ounce of Hal's self-control not to reach over and grab the pencil out of his hand. Ryan closed the sketchbook and handed the pencil back to him. Hal opened his mouth to ask what he was doing, but Ryan held his finger up, mouthing, 'Shhh.' Ryan's eyes flickered to his father, but Gene was loudly insulting the coach of the LA Lakers. Hal gave Ryan a tiny nod and pocketed the sketchbook.

Ryan was staring hard at Hal through his red spectacles, as if he were trying to communicate telepathically. He lifted his right forefinger and pointed it to the ring finger on his left hand. He looked at Hal, to make sure Hal had seen. He crossed his forefingers, making a plus sign, and looked at Hal again. He glanced at his dad, then back to Hal, held up his finger and drew it across his neck.

Hal frowned, baffled by the boy's actions.

'Ah, food,' Uncle Nat said cutting off Gene's rant as Earl approached the table with plates the size of tea trays.

The beef burger made English burgers look like children's portions. Hal needed both hands to lift it, and he couldn't open his mouth wide enough to fit over both halves of the bun. It was delicious though. He looked guiltily at Ryan who was struggling with his food, and puzzled over what the strange boy had tried to tell him.

Ring finger, fingers crossed, and throat cut.

What did it *mean*?

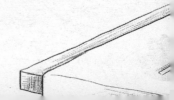

CHAPTER FIVE

THE WILD CARD

Gene gobbled up his lunch, threw down his napkin, and dragged Ryan away from the table before the boy had got halfway through his burger.

'Not sure we've made a brand-new friend there,' Uncle Nat said under his breath as Gene left the dining car with his visibly unhappy son.

'Can we explore the train after we've finished lunch?' Hal asked, stuffing a forkful of salty fries into his mouth. He wondered if he should tell his uncle about Ryan's strange message.

'Why don't you set out on a solo mission? I need to do a bit of work before the press conference.'

'You do?'

Uncle Nat lowered his voice. 'I saw something on August's computer screen when we were in his bedroom and Zola accidentally moved his mouse. She saw it too. Something about a rocket.'

Hal frowned. 'A space rocket?'

'I don't know, but I need to revisit my notes about Reza's interests, make sure I'm prepared for tonight's news. It's going to be big, I can tell. You don't mind, do you?'

'No.' Hal tried to hide his disappointment by finishing his glass of water. He got to his feet. 'I'm going to go and look for Mason and Hadley – give you time to work.'

Following a sign to the 'sightseer lounge', Hal headed out the far end of the dining car, looking for a quiet place to examine Ryan's drawing. He was puzzled by the boy. What had Ryan been trying to tell him? The connecting door hissed open, and he stepped into a dazzlingly bright carriage. Inside, the windows arched up into the roof, and welcoming blue chairs were angled outward to face the grand view.

The train was coasting through a small town. Hal glimpsed backyards with swing sets and lawn furniture. The Comet's famous five-chime horn blasted out a warning, and he heard the bell of a level crossing as they passed over a road. Red and white pickup trucks queued – a child waved from a back seat. Hal raised his hand and waved back.

Someone behind him shoved past.

'Sorry,' Hal said, to the short passenger who was hurrying away. They were dressed oddly, wearing a long grey coat, a baseball cap and sunglasses, and a thick scarf wrapped around their neck.

'Hey, Hal!'

Hal saw Mason sitting in a booth in the centre of the carriage with Hadley. He made his way over, glancing at the rude passenger in the long coat, who was exiting the sightseer lounge through the connecting door.

'What you looking at?' Mason asked, craning his neck.

'Nothing,' Hal replied. 'It's just . . . that person was weird.'

'Weird?' Hadley asked. 'Like, how?'

'They pushed passed me without saying excuse me, and they didn't thank me when I moved.'

'It's not weird for people to have no manners.' Hadley laughed. 'You've obviously never been to a casino.'

'No, I haven't. But that person's wearing a hat, coat and scarf, indoors . . .' Hal frowned. 'It's warm in here.'

'Oh, you meet all sorts of weird and wonderful people on the California Comet.' Mason pulled a face. 'We met you, didn't we?'

'Ha, ha, very funny.' Hal grinned.

'Last time we took the Amtrak, we were sat in coach, and I was next to a world-champion hot-dog eater,' Hadley said, moving up so Hal could sit down beside her. She wrinkled her nose. 'She smelt really funky.'

'What's coach?' Hal asked.

'The cheap seats,' Mason replied. 'Through there, in the next carriage. You sleep sitting up, like on a plane.'

'Are you in coach this time?'

'No.' Hadley did a celebratory shoulder dance. 'We have a family bedroom.'

'Reno pays well,' Mason said, rubbing his hands together.

Hal looked down at the cards spread across the table. 'What're you playing?'

'This is no game,' Hadley said, sweeping the cards into a pile. 'This is magic.' She gave him an intense stare. 'You are lucky enough to be in the presence of the greatest female illusionist in America.' She sighed. 'Or at least I will be one day.'

'You will?'

'Sure. Name a card.'

'Err . . . king of clubs.'

Hadley shuffled the deck, spreading the cards in a fan, face down, across the table. She paused, closed her eyes, and then flipped one of them face up. It was the king of clubs.

'What!' cried Hal as Hadley opened her eyes. 'How did you do that?'

'The cards speak to me,'

Hadley said, her voice mystical. 'Only great magicians can commune with the cards.'

Mason laughed at Hal's astonished expression.

'Great magicians also get thirsty. I'm going to get a drink.' Hadley shimmied out from her seat, accidentally backing into a wiry man in a grey suit. His briefcase clattered to the ground, landing at Hal's feet.

'W-w-watch where you're going!' the man snapped, and Hal recognized him as the man he'd drawn in the dining car – all neck and no chin, his anxious features gathered together beneath slick grey hair.

'Hey!' Mason jumped to his feet. 'Relax, buddy. It was an accident.'

'Your case,' Hal said, picking it up off the floor. The man's name was engraved on a silver plate beside the handle. 'Mr Seymour Hart.'

'Give that b-b-back!' Seymour Hart yanked the case from Hal.

'I . . .' Hal was surprised by the man's anger. 'I *was*.'

Passengers turned their heads and stared.

Seymour Hart hugged the case to his chest and glared at Hadley, who was inadvertently blocking his path. She stepped aside. Hurrying up the aisle, he picked the furthest seat from them possible, beside the door to coach, and sat down in an armchair facing the the window.

'He's from Baltimore,' Mason said.

'How do you know?' Hal asked.

'I can tell by the accent.'

'Jerk,' Hadley said, sucking in her cheeks. Hal could see

she was shaken by the man's anger. 'I'm going downstairs to the cafe. Either of you want a soda?'

'Coke for me,' Mason said as Hal shook his head.

'I can't tell if it's jet lag, or America, or me,' Hal said, returning to his seat as Hadley disappeared down the staircase in the centre of the. 'But I feel like something strange is happening on this train.'

'Relax, it's just some uptight dude with a briefcase,' Mason said.

'No, it's not just him. Things are happening around me . . . I can't explain it.' Hal sighed. 'I feel like I should be able to see something, but I don't know what I'm looking for. It's like an itch but inside my head. Have you ever felt like that?'

'I had lice once,' Mason replied.

Hal laughed. 'Not that kind of itch.'

'You had this feeling before?'

'Only once, but I didn't know what it was at the time.'

'And was something strange happening?'

'Yes – a jewel thief was robbing passengers.'

'Holy cow!' Mason's eyes bulged. 'What happened?'

'I solved the case and caught the thief.'

Mason sat back from the table, staring at Hal. 'You're a detective?'

Hal felt himself blush. 'When I was in the middle of the case, I felt that weird things – invisible things – were happening around me.'

'And you feel that way now?' Mason furtively glanced up and down the sightseer lounge.

Hal nodded. 'But I don't know why.' He leaned forward. 'At lunch, I sat opposite this boy. He was trying to tell me something. He didn't want his dad to see. I think he might be in trouble.'

'What kind of trouble?' Mason's thick eyebrows met as he frowned. 'What was he trying to say?'

'He didn't *say* anything because he has a head brace – the kind that straps round your face and attaches to your teeth.'

'Poor guy. I had braces. They suck.'

'He didn't seem to want to talk, but when I started drawing the dining car, he took my sketchbook and pencil and went over some of the lines I'd drawn. Afterwards he did this series of actions, like he was miming a message . . . but I didn't understand what he meant.'

Hadley reappeared carrying two cans of soda. She slid one across the table to Mason.

'Listen to this, Hadley. Hal's a detective, and some kid with huge braces mimed a secret message to him at lunch.' He pulled the tag and the cola crackled.

'Secret message?' Hadley sat down, slurping from her can. 'Show me. I want to see.'

'He did this, then this, and this.' Hal repeated Ryan's actions. *Ring finger, fingers crossed, and throat cut.* 'And he kept looking nervously at his dad to make sure he didn't see.'

'Which finger did he tap?' asked Hadley.

'This one,' said Hal, pointing. 'The fourth one. I thought it could mean the number four, or . . . it's also the ring finger, so . . .'

Hadley raised her eyebrows. 'So?'

'Maybe he wanted to ring someone?'

'Draw a ring around someone?' Mason looked confused.

'No. You know, telephone someone,' Hal clarified.

'Yeah, we don't say *ring* – we say *call*,' Hadley said.

Hal felt crestfallen, realizing he may not have understood Ryan because he was British.

'It must be the number four,' Mason was saying, as Hal looked up, 'because he did a plus sign next. Hey, it could be a sum. Maybe it's a math problem.'

Hal froze. Gene and Ryan Jackson were walking towards them down the aisle. Gene had a hand on his son's shoulder, driving him forward. '*Shhhhhhhh*,' Hal hissed, grabbing Hadley's deck of cards and hunching forward. Hadley and Mason leaned in.

'What are we doing?' Mason whispered as Hal dealt the cards.

'Let's play gin rummy,' Hal said loudly.

Mason looked confused until he caught sight of Ryan, in his head brace, approaching. Taking her cards, Hadley sat back, clearly trying to steal a sideways view of the Jacksons.

When Hal glanced up, Ryan was staring at him – his eyes pleading – as his father pushed him past the table.

'They're going into coach,' Mason said under his breath. 'I see what you mean about the teeth.'

Hal knew from the look in Ryan's eyes that something was wrong. 'What is it that I'm not seeing?' he hissed.

'Maybe he was threatening you,' Hadley said. 'Like, *you* –'

she pointed at Hal – 'are for –' she pointed at her ring finger and then drew her finger across her throat – '*the chop.*'

'But that leaves the *plus* out.' Hal shook his head.

'You said he drew something in your book,' Mason said. 'Can we see?'

Hal pulled out his sketchbook, flicking to the drawing of the dining car. 'Here.' He pushed it into the middle of the table. 'You see the heavy lines? They're Ryan's. He drew over the edges of tables and walls that I'd already drawn. It makes no sense!'

'Maybe he meant you to see something *in* the picture,' said Hadley, pulling the book closer.

'But *what?*' Hal huffed out an exasperated breath.

'Hey, that's uptight briefcase jerk.' Mason pointed. 'Look, there's his case, under the table. I wonder what he keeps in there that's so precious – diamonds? Forged banknotes?'

'Some of Ryan's lines are part of *his* table . . .' Hal said, thinking out loud. 'The message could be about him.'

'Maybe briefcase jerk is a *murderer!*' Mason drew his finger across his throat.

Dread, like a cold mist, settled on Hal's chest. He didn't know what Ryan was trying to tell him, but something bad was happening on the California Comet.

CHAPTER SIX

THE DEVIL
IN DISGUISE

Unable to work out Ryan's message, they played gin rummy to the soundtrack of the sightseer lounge's rattles and squeaks and the random chatter of passengers. Hadley won every round.

Mason threw his cards down. 'How come you keep winning?' He folded his arms and gave his sister a hard stare. 'Do you have a deck up your sleeves?'

'Are you calling me a cheat?'

'I'm just saying . . .'

There was a thud and someone cried out. Hal turned to look.

The rude passenger in the cap, coat and scarf had tripped over Seymour Hart's briefcase, which had been sticking out into the aisle. The sunglasses and baseball cap had fallen from the passenger's head, revealing blonde hair and a familiar face.

'Marianne?' Hal stood up and then, remembering her earlier behaviour, sat back down.

'I'm s-sorry,' Seymour Hart said, reaching out to help Marianne.

'Get away from me!' She scrambled backwards, grabbing her glasses and cap as she got to her feet. She paused when she saw Hal looking at her, and then hurried towards him.

'I need to talk to you,' she hissed. And, glancing over her shoulder, she added, 'Not here. In the cafe. Make sure no one follows you.' She shot a look at Seymour Hart, then disappeared down the stairs.

Mason and Hadley were looking at Hal with raised eyebrows.

'Friend of yours?' Hadley asked.

'No,' Hal replied. 'I only met her this morning.'

'Hey! You only met *us* this morning!' Mason pretended to be offended.

'So, you gonna go down and talk to her?' Hadley asked.

Hal remembered the look on Marianne's face when she'd screamed at him. 'Will you come with me?'

Mason nodded. 'Sure.'

Downstairs were more booths. Beyond them was a kiosk selling crisps and sweets beside a row of glass-fronted fridges, filled with sandwiches and fizzy drinks. Marianne sat at a table in the corner, furthest from the cafe counter. She'd put the sunglasses and cap back on. Hal walked over, Hadley and Mason following behind.

'Who are *they*?' Marianne asked, looking pointedly over her glasses at Hadley and Mason.

'My friends,' Hal replied.

'I need to talk to you in private.'

'Anything you need to say to me, you can say in front of Mason and Hadley,' Hal insisted.

'Fine.' Marianne looked past them nervously.

Mason slid into the booth opposite her, then Hadley sat down, and Hal, not wanting to sit beside Marianne, perched awkwardly on the end.

'I'm not supposed to be here. If I get caught, I'll be in trouble,' Marianne said. 'I'm not allowed to go anywhere without Woody.'

'Is that why you're wearing the worst disguise ever?' Hadley said, raising a sardonic eyebrow.

'Who's Woody?' Mason asked.

'He's my bodyguard,' Marianne replied haughtily. 'And if this disguise is bad, why didn't Hal recognize me?'

'What do you want, Marianne?' Hal asked flatly.

Her bottom lip trembled. 'I want to say, I'm sorry.'

Hadley looked at Hal.

'What for?'

'For flipping out . . .' Marianne's voice wobbled. 'And hurting you.' She sniffed. 'It's so boring being stuck in my cabin the whole time, and when you came to the Silver Scout, it was fun . . . drawing together . . . I thought we might be friends, and then . . . and then . . . I ruined it.' She hiccupped, and Hal saw a tear roll down her cheek.

'Wait!' Mason looked at Hal. 'You went in the Reza railcar?' He turned to Marianne. 'But, then you must be . . .'

'Mason, Hadley – meet Marianne Reza.'

'You're August Reza's daughter?' Hadley's mouth dropped open. '*The* August Reza . . . of Reza Technologies? The famous billionaire?'

Marianne nodded. 'Hi.'

Mason stared at her, but Marianne ignored him, instead leaning towards Hal. 'I came to apologize.' She pulled off the cap and glasses.

'Does Woody know you left your compartment?'

Marianne shook her head. 'I left music playing. No one will look.'

'That was gutsy.' Hadley sounded impressed.

'I had to find you.' She looked at Hal with wide blue eyes. 'I really am truly sorry for – for hurting you. Forgive me? Please?'

'OK,' Hal said, softening at her apology. 'But, what if your dad looks for you and finds you gone? He'll be worried.'

'*Pfff* – he won't even notice.' She sniffed, wiping her eyes with the back of her hand. 'I get ignored for hours – and anyway, he's busy preparing for tonight's big announcement.'

'Why the disguise?' Mason asked.

'I have a bodyguard for a reason.' Marianne lowered her voice. 'People mustn't recognize me. Did you see that man up there – the one who tripped me with his case? I think he's following me. He saw me get on the train. He was waiting outside the restroom when I came out of the crew cabins. He followed me through the carriages. Didn't you see him coming after me?'

Thinking about it, after Marianne had shoved past him, Hal realized the next person to come down the aisle had been Seymour Hart.

'I hid in coach, and when he didn't come after me, I thought he'd gone away.'

'Why didn't you say something?' Hal asked.

'He called to you –' she pointed at Mason – 'and I wasn't sure you'd want to help me . . . after how horrible I'd been.'

'My name's Mason Moretti.' Mason put a hand to his chest. 'It is an honour to meet you.'

'I shouldn't have come. Woody always tells me it's too risky for me to be out alone. It was a mistake.'

'Are you sure that man is after you?' Hal asked.

Marianne nodded. 'He looks like the guy who was arrested for stalking me back in Silicon Valley. Hal, I'm frightened.'

Hadley nodded. 'He's one angry jerk. But why would he follow you?'

'There are plenty of people who want to steal my father's

secrets or get their hands on his money. Sometimes, they try to get to him through me.' She looked at Hal. 'Once, a woman came to my school pretending to be a teacher. She was asking all these questions about my father. When I told the principal, it turned out she wasn't a teacher. She was just pretending to be one. She was a spy who worked for Zircona.' She sat back. 'They arrested her. But that's why we have Woody now. It's his job to protect me.' She bit her lip. 'Except he thinks I'm safe in my cabin.' She looked at all three of them. 'And I'm scared that the man upstairs is another Zircona spy.'

'What's Zircona?' asked Hal.

'The Zircona Corporation? They're only, like, the biggest company in the world,' Mason said, sounding incredulous.

'Third biggest,' Marianne corrected him. 'Reza Technologies is the second biggest. Zircona is my father's rival.'

'The rivalry between Zircona and Reza is famous,' Hadley said to Hal. 'There's always stories about it in the papers.'

'My father is paranoid that someone from Zircona will kidnap me.'

'By the sounds of it, he might be right,' Mason said.

'Well, at least then maybe he'd notice me,' Marianne said bitterly.

'I think you should go back to the Silver Scout,' Hal said. 'I don't know anything about Reza Technologies or Zircona, or how big businesses work, but if you are in danger, then we need to get you back to your railcar, where you're safe.'

'Do you forgive me, Hal?' Marianne asked hopefully. 'I couldn't stand it if you hated me.'

'I don't hate you,' Hal replied with a half-smile.

'So, we're friends again?'

'We're friends,' Hal said.

Marianne leaned over the table and kissed his forehead. 'Oh thank you,' she gushed as Hal turned red.

'Next stop is Mount Pleasant,' Hadley said, studying the timetable on the wall. 'The train takes on luggage there, so you'll have plenty of time to get back to the Silver Scout.'

'But if Seymour Hart sees Marianne get off the train, he might try and get to her,' said Mason, clearly excited by the drama.

'We'll walk you back to your railcar, Marianne,' Hal said. 'Make sure you're safe.'

'I've got a better idea,' Marianne said.

Two minutes later, Hadley came out of the restroom wearing Marianne's cap, scarf and sunglasses. She twirled in the long coat. 'How do I look?'

Marianne, who was now wearing Hadley's purple hoodie, giggled. 'You look like you're wearing a terrible disguise!'

'Promise me you'll give me my sweater back when we're done,' Hadley said. 'It was a birthday present from my dad.'

'I promise.'

'Train's slowing down,' Mason said, squishing his face against the window.

'I'm gonna lead that Zircona spy on the wildest goose chase.' Hadley flashed them a wicked grin.

'Be careful, sis,' Mason said.

'I'll be fine.' Hadley waved his caution away. 'Meet you

back in our bedroom.' And she climbed the stairs.

'There's no exit door in this carriage or the dining car,' Hal said. 'The quickest way to get off the train is to go into coach, down the stairs and out that door.'

'But we'll have to pass the spy,' Mason said.

'Not if he's taken the bait and followed Hadley.'

Sure enough, when Hal peeped round the top of the staircase, Seymour Hart was gone. 'The coast's clear.'

'Let's get this done,' Mason said, barging past him and into coach. 'I want to make sure my sister's all right.'

Hurrying through coach, Hal spotted the lady he'd drawn in Chicago station. She was still wearing her blue puffer coat, but her lizard was on her lap now, and she was tickling its chin. After running down the stairs, Hal jumped onto the platform feeling a thrill of excitement as he drew in a lungful of crisp autumn air.

'It worked.' Marianne glanced over her shoulder as they half ran, half jogged towards the Silver Scout. Stepping up to the door, she typed numbers into a keypad. 'Thank you for helping me,' she said, breathless now. She looked at Hal. 'And for forgiving me. Mason, tell Hadley she'll get her sweater back tomorrow.' The door was open. '*À bientôt.*' She gave them a little wave, climbed into the carriage, and shut the door behind her.

CHAPTER SEVEN

THE MORETTI MAGIC SHOW

A gust of wind whirled dead leaves into the air, and Hal shivered. The boys boarded the California Comet through the first open door and made their way up the stairs.

'That's my roomette,' Hal said. 'Number ten.'

Glancing in, they saw Uncle Nat bent over his notebook.

'Hi, Francine,' Hal said to the smiling attendant, as they passed into the next carriage.

'An Amtrak friend is a friend for life!' Francine called after them.

'This is us.' Mason pointed at a door, but then called out, 'Hadley!' as his sister came towards them, unwinding Marianne's scarf from her neck.

'Were you followed?' Hal asked.

She shook her head. 'When I got upstairs, the Zircona spy was gone.' She slid the compartment door open. 'Did he follow you?'

'Nope, and Marianne's back in her fancy carriage now,' Mason said.

Hal looked through the open door. Their bedroom was large compared to his roomette. On the sofa, there was a half-empty suitcase, and clothes were strewn everywhere.

'Did your luggage explode?' Hal asked, looking around.

'Mason couldn't find his voice recorder,' Hadley explained, gathering up an armful of clothes and dumping them into the suitcase.

The compartment had a shower room, and tucked in the corner was a wide seat, like the ones in Hal's roomette, covered with bags and books about performing magic.

'You really do want to be a magician, then?' Hal said, picking one up.

'Yeah.' Hadley nodded. 'Where Mom lives, in Boston, there's an annual talent competition. The prize is five thousand dollars. This year I'm old enough to enter. If I win, we're going to buy some big stage tricks . . .'

'. . . and launch *The Moretti Magic Show*,' Mason finished.

'You're both in it?'

'Yeah. I do the magic. Mason does impressions. Want to see us do a trick?' Hadley asked, pushing Hal towards the cluttered chair. 'Sit there.'

Mason swept the suitcase on to the floor, pulling the sofa out to turn the double bed into a stage. Hal perched on the arm of the chair as Hadley lifted a rainbow-sequinned jacket out of a bag and slipped it on. Opening the wardrobe, Mason took out a gold dress and blonde wig. Wriggling out of his tracksuit bottoms, he pulled on the dress and then the wig.

'Hadley's the world's best illusionist, and I'm –' he primped the blonde hair and put on a feminine voice – 'her glamorous assistant.'

Hal laughed as Mason clambered on to the bed and stood beside his sister, gesturing to her dramatically as if she were a grand prize.

'Ladies and gentleman, my name is Hadley Moretti, master illusionist. And this is Marilyn Mason, my glamorous assistant.' Hal grinned as Mason waved flirtatiously. 'What you're about to see defies the laws of science . . .'

'. . . and bamboozles me,' Mason said in a high cutesy voice.

'Before your very eyes –' Hadley pulled a black square of cloth from her pocket – 'I will make Marilyn disappear.' She unfolded the square, again and again, until it was blanket-sized. Stepping forward, she held it at knee height, and Mason started singing '*Happy birthday to you*' in a high breathy voice. Slowly and dramatically she lifted the cloth. Mason kept singing, blowing Hal a kiss before he was totally hidden. As Mason sang the last refrain of the song – '. . . *Happy birthday to you*' – Hadley dropped the cloth, and he was gone.

Hal sat up, looking around the tiny bedroom. He blinked, trying to work out what had happened. Mason had vanished.

Hadley made a show of picking up the cloth, searching it, turning it this way and that. It developed a bulge, and she lifted out a crystal ball from its folds. 'Hold this for me, would you?' She threw the crystal ball to Hal, whipping the cloth out to its full size and holding it up, dropping it to the ground again, and there, standing beside her, blowing bubbles at Hal, was Mason.

Hal leaped to his feet, clapping, as Mason took his sister's hand and they both curtsied. 'How d'you do that? It was amazing.'

'Really?' Mason pulled the wig off his head. 'You didn't see how it was done?'

'You should see our other tricks.' Hadley beamed. 'We've got one where Mason sings country songs while I saw him in half.'

Hal laughed. 'I'd buy a ticket.'

'Hi, kids!' The door to the compartment opened, and a short man wearing a Hawaiian shirt and beige chinos entered. His curly black hair receded to a bald pate, and merry brown eyes bulged out of his face.

'Pop,' said Mason, throwing his blond wig back in the duffel bag. 'Meet Hal. He's British!'

'Good to meet you, Hal. I'm Frank.' He shook Hal's hand enthusiastically. 'Have they been practising on you? Because, you know you can charge for that? It's hard work, all that clapping.'

Hal grinned, liking the jovial man immediately.

Frank looked about. 'What on earth happened in here?'

'We were about to tidy up.' Hadley looked at the floor guiltily.

'I need my razor.' Frank rubbed his hand over his chin. 'There's a gorgeous redhead in the dining car – got a pet lizard. Her name is Adie, and I think I might be her type.' He winked. 'Grab my washbag, son.' He filled the sink with water. 'Time for a shave.'

'Got it.' Mason pulled out shaving foam and a razor, and

squirted a ball of foam into his dad's outstretched hand.

Rubbing his palms together, Frank patted the white lather on to his chin. 'So, whereabouts you from in Britain, Hal?'

'Crewe,' said Hal. 'It's a railway town.'

'You like trains?' Frank rinsed his hands and took the razor. 'We love trains, don't we, kids?'

Hadley and Mason made grumbling noises.

'My job takes me all over the country,' said Frank, pausing to shave one cheek, 'and I can't drive, on account of a misunderstanding.'

'It's called a speeding ticket,' Mason said.

'Four speeding tickets,' Hadley clarified.

'They were emergencies!' Frank protested.

'I thought everyone in America flew,' Hal said.

'Flying ain't natural unless you're a bird,' Frank said, leaning towards the mirror and pulling the razor up his neck. 'Anyway, I prefer a train.'

Hal nodded; he felt the same.

'I'm telling you I've got a good feeling about Reno, kids. This gig's gonna be the one that gets me a residency. Then you can go to a proper school, and I won't have to pay for a tutor.' He dropped his razor into the sink and took the hand towel Hadley held out. 'Thanks, chipmunk.' He dabbed it to his neck. 'How do I look?'

'Irresistible,' Hadley replied as her dad slapped on a strong-smelling aftershave. 'Adie and her pet lizard won't know what's hit them.'

Frank pointed at his reflection in the mirror, snarled his top lip and said '*Uh-huh!*' then left, calling over his shoulder, 'See you in the dining car – hopefully I'll have a lady friend with me.'

Hal's eyes settled on the sink, the ring of soap suds and the discarded razor. A sequence of images played through his head, and he gasped. 'Razor. *Razor!*' He looked at Hadley and Mason. Tapping his ring finger, he said, 'Marry . . .' He made a plus sign with his fingers. 'And . . .' He mimed shaving his neck. 'Razor! . . . Marry and razor . . . *Marianne Reza.*'

'Whoa!' Mason's eyes widened. 'That means . . . Wait – what does it mean?'

Hadley frowned. 'Hang on, does Ryan even know Marianne?'

'It doesn't seem likely,' Hal said.

'Maybe his dad is a Zircona spy too,' Mason suggested.

'Gene Jackson doesn't seem the kind of man who works for a technology company.' Hal shook his head.

'Why did he give *you* the message?' Hadley wondered.

'Uncle Nat told Gene that we'd met August Reza and been in the Silver Scout that morning. Ryan must've thought I knew her.' Hal felt a prickle of excitement.

'You *do* know her,' Mason pointed out.

'Maybe he drew those lines around Seymour Hart's table,' Hadley said, her eyes widening, 'because he'd discovered the man was after Marianne.'

'But how?' Hal asked, glad of the Morettis' help with this puzzle.

'It can't be a coincidence that Ryan draws lines around Seymour Hart, and then we find out he's stalking Marianne,' Mason said.

Hal nodded. 'I'm worried about her.'

'She's in her private railcar with her bodyguard,' Hadley reminded him. 'She's safe.'

'For now,' said Hal.

'So, what do we do?' Hadley asked.

'We need to talk to Ryan, ask him about the message.'

'Wanna have dinner with us?' Mason asked. 'We might see him in the dining car.'

'Dinner!' Hal exclaimed, suddenly remembering his appointment with Zola. 'I can't, I've got to go. Let's meet after the press conference.'

CHAPTER EIGHT

THE ZIRCONA QUESTION

'I'm back,' Hal said, poking his head into the roomette.

'I was about to send out a search party,' Uncle Nat replied, rifling through his bag and pulling out a knitted silk tie. 'I'm just putting this on for dinner.'

'I don't have to wear one, do I?'

'No. It's just . . . Zola has this way of making me feel underdressed.'

'But you always look good.'

Uncle Nat straightened up. 'That's a kind thing to say.' He smiled. 'Perhaps you're right.' He put the tie away. 'We'll go as we are. Are you ready? Zola says we are to stop by her compartment for pre-dinner drinks.'

'Do I have to come?' Hal stepped back to let Uncle Nat out of the roomette.

'You're the reason Zola's invited us to dinner.'

Hal fell into step beside his uncle. 'What if I say something I shouldn't?'

'Don't worry. And if Zola asks you questions that make you uncomfortable, change the subject.'

Hal put his hand in his pocket and felt his sketchbook. If he got a moment, he wanted to draw Hadley and Mason in their *Moretti Magic Show* costumes, while the vision was fresh in his mind.

'Here we are. Bedroom B.' Uncle Nat knocked, then straightened his jacket.

The door slid open. Zola greeted them with a smile. She had changed into black trousers and a white blouse with a scooped neckline. Her high heels were the same red as her lips. 'Welcome, welcome. Do sit down.'

Zola had transformed the functional blue bedroom into a stylish sitting room. An ochre scarf encased the fluorescent ceiling light, softening its harsh glow, and a maroon throw covered the sofa, topped by a scattering of gold cushions.

'You brought cushions?' Uncle Nat said as he sat down.

'I brought cushion *cases*. I keep my nightclothes in them.' She picked up a silver cocktail shaker. 'Let me fix you a drink.'

'What's that smell?' asked Hal, sitting in an armchair draped with a cherry-red pashmina.

'Sandalwood,' said Zola, 'from my diffuser. A few drops of oil and I can make anywhere smell like home. Harrison, have you ever tried a *diabolo menthe*?' Hal shook his head. 'Oh, you should.'

71

Opening a cupboard, she took out a small bottle of bright green liquid, poured it into a glass, and handed it to him.

Hal eyed the fizzing liquid cautiously. The last green drink he'd been given had been disgusting.

'It's peppermint soda,' Zola said, and Hal nodded, smiling politely as she poured clear liquid into a silver shaker, added a handful of ice, and rattled it vigorously. 'I read all about your

brilliant detective work on the case of the Highland Falcon Thief.' She poured the mixture into two glasses.

'You did?' Hal was surprised.

'Yes. In the newspaper.' She locked eyes with him. 'Very impressive.' She opened a jar, skewered olives on to two cocktail sticks and dropped them into each drink with a soft *plunk*. 'How clever to outsmart an ingenious criminal by using your skill as an artist.' She passed Uncle Nat his drink without taking her eyes from Hal. 'To Harrison Beck, the railway detective.' She lifted her glass.

'To my clever nephew,' said Uncle Nat, grinning at Hal, who could feel himself blushing.

'Do you have a sketchbook with you on this trip?' Zola took a sip of her drink. 'I'd love to see some of your pictures.'

'You will have already seen some of Hal's pictures – in the papers,' Uncle Nat said drily.

'I meant of the California Comet. Have you drawn it? What about the Silver Scout? Did you draw anything after our little visit? The toy train perhaps?'

Hal was uncomfortably aware of the sketchbook in his pocket and took a swig of the green drink to avoid answering. It was frothy and tasted like toothpaste. He winced and swallowed.

'Why the interest in Reza's model train?' Uncle Nat asked.

'Did you know that Reza has been buying up land in the Northeast Corridor?' Zola said, slipping off her heels and curling up on the sofa. 'Now why would he do that, do you think?'

73

'At first I thought he was planning to build a high-speed railway –' Uncle Nat leaned towards her – 'but then we saw . . .'

'. . . that document about a *rocket* on his computer.' She gave him a meaningful look. 'Space travel.'

Uncle Nat shrugged. 'August Reza's never shown any interest in space travel before.'

'That's why I wanted to see the drawings.' She looked at Hal. 'Was there a rocket station or launcher in that toy train set?'

'August Reza only talked about trains.' Hal replied, wondering if he could make an excuse to go to the bathroom and pour away the minty drink.

Zola's smartwatch flashed with a message, which she brushed away with a manicured finger.

'I don't know how you can wear one of those things.' Uncle Nat shook his head. 'I'd hate being permanently plugged in and pestered. Disconnecting from normal life is one of the most appealing things about travelling.'

'I like to be connected to the world. It keeps me on top of my game.' Zola chuckled. 'You're an old-fashioned soul, with your ink pens and handwritten journals.'

'How would Zircona react to Reza Technologies getting into space travel?' Hal asked, thinking about Marianne.

Zola turned and stared at Hal. 'What makes you ask *that* question?'

'I . . . I . . . don't know. I-I don't even know what Zircona do,' Hal spluttered. 'But they're rivals, aren't they? Zircona and Reza?' He shrugged and peered into his green

74

drink to avoid Zola's penetrating look.

'Zircona trade in digital information,' said Uncle Nat, studying Zola with apparent interest. 'They own software and hardware companies. If I'm not mistaken, they made the watch Zola's wearing.'

'It's very clever.' Zola held up her wrist. 'It seems to know what I want to know before I know it myself.' Her laugh was low and sultry.

'Are Zircona interested in space travel?' Hal asked.

'No,' Zola replied. 'Zircona have invested billions in self-driving cars.'

'Robot cars?'

'Yes. In the future, a Zircona car will pick you up at your door and take you where you need to go. There'll be no need for trains.' Zola took the empty cocktail glasses and rinsed them in the little sink. 'The car has always eclipsed the train.'

'And yet the train has endured,' said Uncle Nat quietly.

'How was the drink?' Zola asked Hal.

'Mmmm, um, minty.'

'I used to drink them when I was at university in Paris.'

'That's where Marianne goes to school,' Hal said.

'She's a smart cookie. Probably end up running Reza Technologies one day. Are you two friends?'

Hal realized he was nodding only when it was too late to stop, and he could tell by the triumphant look on Zola's face that he'd given something away.

'How convenient for your uncle!' Zola arched an eyebrow at Uncle Nat.

'I don't understand.' Hal frowned.

'Look –' she crossed her arms – 'I'm not buying this cute English *we're here on holiday because we love trains* act.'

Hal was flabbergasted by her outburst and looked at his uncle, who laughed.

'Zola thinks I have brought you on this trip to turn your excellent observation skills to my advantage. That I've asked you to work your way into the Reza family and feed me any juicy nuggets you uncover, while sketching everything you see.'

'Oh!' Hal sat up. 'Do you want me to? Because I will if . . .'

'No, Hal.' Uncle Nat shook his head. 'This trip is a birthday present.' He turned to Zola. 'We discovered on the Highland Falcon that we do genuinely love riding trains together.'

Hal glowed with pleasure and nodded vigorously. 'I'm not just friends with Marianne. I've also made friends with a boy who does impressions and a girl who does magic, and they're no use to Uncle Nat at all.'

Zola looked unconvinced. 'Well, I've got my eyes on you two.' She pointed to each of them and Hal felt flattered.

'I'm covering the press conference for the *Telegraph*,' Uncle Nat said. 'But you haven't said who *you're* working for.'

'I'm a simple girl with an appetite for corporate risk and industry disruption.' Zola fluttered her eyelashes. 'A new area of expansion for Reza Technologies is a big story.'

'You're hoping to uncover some big secret and sell the story to the highest bidder?'

'You say that like it's a bad thing.' She pouted cheekily,

and Uncle Nat laughed. Her watch flashed an alert. 'Time for dinner – if we want to eat and prepare for the press conference.' She pressed a button. 'And I hope you packed an umbrella because my watch says it's going to rain.'

Uncle Nat looked out the window. 'The sky disagrees.'

'Technology is the future, Nathaniel,' said Zola, picking up her handbag and opening the door. 'If you don't move with the times, you'll be left behind.'

'Trains are the future, Zola,' Uncle Nat said, getting to his feet, 'and I've never missed one.'

CHAPTER NINE

REZA'S ROCKET

As the California Comet rumbled out of Iowa and into the state of Nebraska, Hal turned from Uncle Nat and Zola's dinner conversation to watch the big orange sun set into the Missouri River. *It looks like it's having a dip*, he thought.

Omaha station was on the east side of the city, nestled between buildings. On the far side of the tracks, a pathway marked with lanterns stretched across the dusty ground towards a grand building illuminated by spotlights. 'That's the Durham Museum,' Uncle Nat said, looking over his shoulder, 'where the press conference will be.'

Zola got up from the table. 'August said the conference will be in two parts. Drinks in the museum, for the big announcement, and then we all have to look at old trains.' She mimed yawning. 'Afterwards, in the Silver Scout, he says he's going to show us something revolutionary.' She lowered her voice. 'Bet it's the rocket.'

After nipping back to the roomette to get their coats, Hal and Uncle Nat joined the rest of the invited journalists, who were gathered on the platform.

'This way, everyone, please,' chirruped an enthusiastic woman with bouncy hair, waving a clipboard, shepherding them along the platform to the back of the train.

Passengers looked down at them from the train windows. Hal spotted Mason and Hadley waving madly, and he saluted back feeling very grown-up. Following the group around the corrugated curve of the Silver Scout, Hal saw that boards had been laid over the rails. They were led across the tracks to the lantern-lit path.

'Omaha was the start of the First Transcontinental Railroad,' Uncle Nat said. 'Once, this was one of the busiest stations in the country.' He sighed. 'Now this beautiful station is a museum.'

'Then what are these tracks used for?' Hal pointed to the rails.

'Freight trains, mostly, and the California Comet stop is over there, but Omaha station is a shadow of what it used to be. I would've loved to have seen it in its heyday.'

They entered the museum through a back door, passing an exhibition space containing an old black train carriage, and arriving in an enormous hall to the sound of a string quartet.

'It looks like Union Station,' Hal said, staring at the ornate ceiling.

'It *is* Union Station – or was,' Uncle Nat said. 'Union Pacific are one of the largest railway companies in America. Their headquarters are in Omaha. This was the first and grandest of the stations they built. Eight different railway companies came

79

to use it. It's the heart of America's railways, old and new.'

'Are you sure this press conference is going to be about a rocket?' Hal asked, looking around. 'Everything here is about trains.'

The hall was buzzing. Television cameras and microphones were dotted about. Several people came up to Uncle Nat and shook his hand. Hal smiled politely and nodded when he was introduced, but he was itching to go and see the old American locomotives.

A hush spread through the crowd as August Reza made his way to a podium. A rush of applause greeted him, and Hal moved to get a clear view.

'Thank you for being here today.' Reza clasped the podium and surveyed the room with an energetic grin. Behind him stood Marianne, in a bright yellow dress, looking bored. 'Today we stand on the brink of a revolution. The climate is changing, and we, as the most adaptable species on earth, will change with it.

'Two hundred years ago, a man called Robert Stephenson made a machine that changed the world. Stephenson's Rocket was the most advanced and practical steam engine of its day. Its whistle heralded the industrial revolution.

'Today, here, now, I'm announcing a competition.'

A murmur rippled through the crowd.

'A competition to find the most innovative prototype of a clean energy locomotive and rail system, as revolutionary as Stephenson's Rocket. Entries are open to anyone anywhere in the world.' He looked down the barrel of a nearby camera.

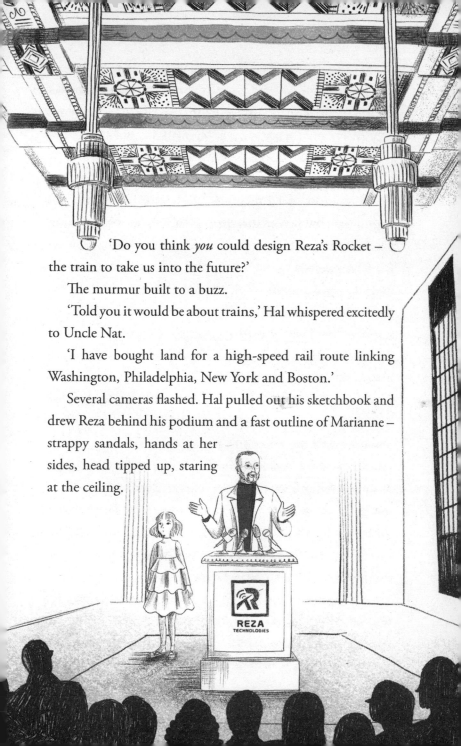

'Do you think *you* could design Reza's Rocket – the train to take us into the future?'

The murmur built to a buzz.

'Told you it would be about trains,' Hal whispered excitedly to Uncle Nat.

'I have bought land for a high-speed rail route linking Washington, Philadelphia, New York and Boston.'

Several cameras flashed. Hal pulled out his sketchbook and drew Reza behind his podium and a fast outline of Marianne – strappy sandals, hands at her sides, head tipped up, staring at the ceiling.

'I'm committing twenty per cent of my company's annual profits to this enterprise, as well as our newest technology: the Reza Solar Storage Battery. It's the smallest, most powerful solar energy storage battery ever invented. I'll be showing it to you later.'

More camera flashes and some hands went up.

'Without the need to pay for fuel, we'll be able to offer high-speed travel at an affordable price.' He raised his hands. 'Oh, and I almost forgot. The prize for the competition winner is a billion dollars.'

Hal gasped and the room erupted. People were calling out August Reza's name and waving to ask questions. Uncle Nat surged forward with the other journalists.

Watching the back-and-forth of questions and answers about batteries and business, Hal lost interest in the press conference. Looking at the big doors leading into the museum, he decided it would be nice to see the trains alone, without the crowd.

He crossed the room and pushed the door open. On the other side was a hall with railway tracks set into the floor. Sitting on the rails were beautiful old carriages. Hal was drawn to them – it was quiet in there. Passing two sunny-yellow carriages with *Union Pacific* painted in red, he saw that one had *PULLMAN* spelled out on the side and smiled. It was comforting to be so far from home yet see something familiar. A forest-green carriage at the end of the platform looked like the grand ones on the Highland Falcon. The wooden bench opposite felt like an invitation to draw. He sat down, flicked to a clean page in his sketchbook, and, without looking down, he captured the refined lines of the carriage. He lovingly recorded the rounded edges and raised ridge of the roof, remembering the time he'd scrambled across a similar roof on a moving train.

Glancing down at his drawing, Hal cried out. White grooves were scored into the page, ruining his picture. He would have to start again on a new page. He remembered Ryan pressing the pencil hard as he drew and wondered angrily how many pages were ruined. He ran his finger over the grooves. *There's a pattern to the lines!* he thought. Quickly, he brushed the flat edge of his pencil point across the paper, shading over the indentations. A word appeared.

HELP.

Hal's heart jumped. He flipped back to the drawing of the dining car – there was Seymour Hart – and played through the scene in his head. Ryan had drawn the lines, passed the book back to him . . . and then mimed Marianne Reza's name.

Help. Marianne Reza.

A chill shook him. He heard the distant sound of applause and snapped his book shut, leaping up and rushing back to the hall.

'There you are!' Uncle Nat clapped a hand on his shoulder, but his expression became concerned when he saw Hal's face. 'Are you all right?'

'Where's Marianne?' Hal looked through the crowd to the stage. She'd gone.

'She's with her father,' Uncle Nat said. 'What on earth's the matter?'

'I think Marianne's in danger,' Hal said, wondering how to

explain Ryan's strange message without it sounding like a silly game. 'Can we go outside?'

Uncle Nat nodded, and they moved through the crowd, out of the museum and on to the lantern-lit path. The sky above the Silver Scout was the colour of a purple bruise. It would soon be dark.

'Marianne told me that there are people after her.'

'And you believe her?' Uncle Nat asked, looking worried.

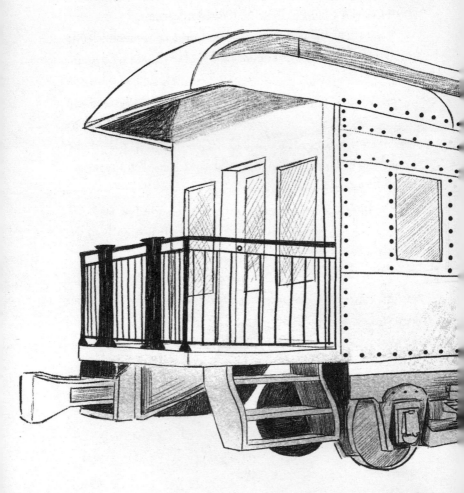

'Well . . .' Hal thought about how oddly Marianne behaved. He didn't trust her entirely, but Ryan's message couldn't be ignored. 'There have been some strange things happening on the train.'

'Marianne has a personal bodyguard,' Uncle Nat said, trying to reassure him. 'I'm sure she's quite safe.'

'I know, but I've got this horrible feeling . . .' Hal's hand went to his chest.

'How can I help?' Uncle Nat asked in earnest.

'I need to go back to the train and ask someone some questions before I can be certain,' Hal said, thinking of Ryan. 'Would you find Marianne and keep an eye on her for me? I know she has Woody, but I'd feel better if you were watching her too.'

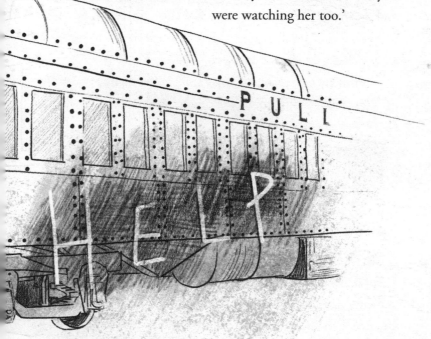

He didn't tell his uncle that Marianne had sneaked away from Woody once already.

'Of course.' Uncle Nat nodded. 'Reza's presentation about the solar battery is happening in the Silver Scout. She's probably in there. I'm sure no one will mind if I skip the museum tour and show up early. I'll bet that's what Zola's done. But you mustn't worry, Hal. Marianne is quite safe.'

'Thanks,' Hal said with a grateful smile. 'I'll come and find you when I'm done.' He ran across the boards, round the Silver Scout, and stepped up on to the platform. He had no idea where on the train Ryan and Gene were seated, but he'd seen them go into coach, and so he boarded the train there and worked his way through the carriage, then the sightseer lounge and the dining car, scanning the passengers. There was no sign of them. Realizing they might be in a bedroom or a roomette, he knocked on each and every door, asking for Ryan.

Eventually he arrived at Mason and Hadley's compartment.

Mason opened the door wearing a false moustache. 'Hey! What was the museum like?'

Hadley was wearing her rainbow-sequined jacket. 'What's up?'

Hal held up his sketchbook. '*Look!*'

'*HELP!* . . . What does that mean?' Hadley asked.

'Ryan made these marks, through the page, with my pencil. It's an invisible message. I only saw it when I tried to draw over it.' Hal looked from Hadley to Mason. 'He was trying to tell me that Marianne Reza is in danger. He was saying, *Help –*' he pointed at the page and then did the actions – '*Marianne Reza.*'

'Wow.' Mason sat down, peeling off the moustache. 'What kind of danger?'

'I don't know. Seymour Hart's in this picture, so he could have something to do with it, but he might not . . .' Hal's pulse was racing. 'I've looked everywhere for Ryan. I need to know what he meant, but I don't know if he's in a roomette or . . .'

'He's next door,' Hadley said.

'What?'

'Ryan and his mean dad are in the bedroom next door.' Mason nodded. 'We saw them come out for dinner.'

Hal dashed into the corridor and banged on their door. There was no answer.

'Where's Marianne now?' asked Hadley from the doorway.

'In the Silver Scout. My uncle's keeping an eye on her.'

'If you can't find Ryan, maybe we should go talk to her?'

'And tell her what? That she's in danger?' Mason asked. 'She's the one who told that to us!'

'Yeah, well –' Hadley pulled off her jacket and grabbed a cardigan – 'I'd want to know about Ryan's message. Wouldn't you?'

'Let's go,' Hal said.

The three of them burst out on to the platform. The dirty yellow strip-lights overhead were dimly reflected by the Comet's carriages.

As they approached the Silver Scout, Hal saw Zola stepping out on to the platform. He opened his mouth to call out to her, but before he could, a high-pitched scream cut through the night.

Hal exploded forward, sprinting past the corner of the station building. He saw a figure in a yellow dress struggling, being dragged backwards by a hooded figure.

'Marianne!' Hal shouted. She was thrashing about, her blonde hair flying. The dark figure bundled her into the boot of a car, slamming it shut and muting her screams.

'Stop!' Hal shouted, as he raced towards the car. Zola was running too, impressively fast in her high heels. Uncle Nat was suddenly there, overtaking Zola. He could hear Mason and Hadley right behind him. There was a shout from Woody.

The hooded figure jumped into the driver's seat. The engine was already running. The tyres squealed and the car lurched away from them into the night.

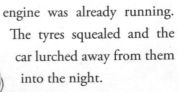

CHAPTER TEN

SHERLOCK DA VINCI

'Help!' Zola shrieked, pivoting and running back to the Silver Scout. 'We need *help*!'

Uncle Nat vaulted over the low fence, sprinting after the car as it sped away. Woody was right behind him. Mason chased after them.

Hal dropped to his knees, ripping his sketchbook from his pocket and slamming it down on to the tarmac, scrabbling for a clean page. His fingers gripped the pencil so hard, the lines didn't flow. He took a breath and tried to calm the fear racing around his body. The car took shape on the page, scuffed and dented, the number plate in his mind's eye. A stripe across the top; the word *Ohio*; then three words *Birthplace of Aviation*; the letters *FWW*; and then four numbers, *983#* . . . The fourth number wasn't there. It had been scratched out. He took another breath and focused on the dark figure dragging Marianne backwards. He closed his eyes. He noted the height difference, the shape of the body, Marianne's posture, their feet.

Hadley stood over him, watching silently.

Hal finished and stared down at his picture.

'What's that?' Hadley tapped him on the shoulder and pointed at a car.

Hal looked and saw a white piece of paper tucked under the windscreen wiper of the vehicle next to the car that had taken Marianne away. Hadley ran over to it.

A crowd of alarmed and curious journalists burst out of the Silver Scout behind a distressed August Reza. There was a hubbub as everyone asked questions at once. Zola stood before Marianne's dad, breathless and visibly upset.

'She was taken. Your daughter. There was a man, in a car, over there.' She pointed to the car park. 'They've gone. Oh August, she's been kidnapped.'

'*Marianne!*' August Reza cried, lurching forward, running into the car park, looking about wildly as if he might be able to see his daughter. 'Marianne?' he called into the night. '*Marianne!*'

Hal felt sick. Why hadn't Uncle Nat been watching her like he'd promised? What had happened to Woody?

Uncle Nat ran back into the car park, followed by Mason. He went straight to August Reza. 'The car turned right into Pacific Street, then went north on South 10th Street.' He gasped. 'It was a Chevy. Dark red – maroon. I couldn't get the plate.' He paused to catch his breath, and Hal heard sirens. 'Woody called 911.'

August Reza turned in a circle, not knowing what to do, he looked up and howled in helpless anger at the night sky. 'Marianne!'

Hadley waved Hal over to the car. 'It's a ransom note!' she hissed. Hal saw a message written with cut-out newspaper letters. 'We mustn't touch it. It might have fingerprints on it.'

Hal nodded and quickly copied the message into his sketchbook. He felt like he might throw up as he wrote down the cruel words. 'Uncle Nat,' he called out, 'there's a note here for Mr Reza.' He pointed at the windscreen.

Woody came running back into the car park, ashen-faced.

'Where is she?' August shouted at him. '*WHERE IS SHE?*'

Woody shook his head, and lifted his empty hands. 'I took my eye off her for one minute. She wanted a drink . . .'

'You're fired!' August shouted, turning away from the bodyguard. 'No.' He turned back. 'You're not fired. You're not going to rest till we've found my little Mari and brought her home safely. *Then* you're fired.'

Woody looked at the ground, and Hal saw a pained expression on his face.

'Get everyone away from here and into the station till the police come. No one is leaving.'

'August, come here, you need to see this,' said Uncle Nat.

'Ransom note?' August's voice was abrupt as he struggled to contain his emotions.

Hal nodded and stepped back to let him read it.

'Don't touch it, sir,' Hadley said softly, 'in case of fingerprints.'

He scanned the paper without lifting the wiper. 'Greedy lowlifes!' His voice was a rasp, and with a yell he raised clenched fists and brought them down on the bonnet of the car with a bang.

'They won't get far,' Uncle Nat said with quiet certainty. 'The police will find her.'

The night blazed with red and blue lights as a squadron of police cars pulled into the car park. August Reza stepped out to meet them, a lone silhouette.

'Hal, are you OK?' Uncle Nat put an arm around his shoulders.

Hal shrugged it off. 'You were supposed to be watching her.' He felt a surge of anger. 'Didn't you believe me?'

'I did. I thought she was safe, in the Silver Scout. I took my eyes off her only for a minute . . .' Hal looked away. 'I'm so sorry.' He put his hand on Hal's arm, and Hal felt himself shaking.

'I got the number plate,' he said gruffly, his voice thick with emotion.

'Really?'

'Yes. The car had a dent in the rear-right fender, and the tyres were almost bald. The person dragging Marianne backwards was short, only three or four inches taller than Marianne. They were dressed in black, so it's hard to say, but, well, I think it was a woman.'

'What! Why?'

'I can't be certain. I couldn't see her hair or face as she had on a balaclava and a black hoodie, but her feet looked small, about the same size as Marianne's. We should see if there are footprints in the dirt. The thing that gave her away was the shape of her body, the waist and the curve of hips.' Hal nodded. 'Yes. I'm certain, it was a woman.'

Mason and Hadley, who were standing nearby, listened to the exchange with their mouths open.

'How did you see all of that?' Hadley asked as Uncle Nat guided the three children towards the squat flat-roofed station.

Hal shrugged. 'I look at the shape, size and scale of things when I'm drawing. It's like my brain takes a photo of something, and then my hand is the printer. I don't notice details though until I'm drawing them. If I talk before I draw, if you ask me to describe something with words, my memory gets blurred and I'm not certain of what I saw.'

'Dude!' Mason exclaimed. 'You're like Leonardo da Vinci and Sherlock Holmes rolled into one.'

'I'm not,' Hal replied feelingly. 'Sherlock Holmes would have worked everything out before Marianne was kidnapped.'

Faces gathered in the windows of the Comet like bunches of balloons. Passengers pressed their noses to the glass trying to see what was going on.

Hal, Mason and Hadley went into the station, finding it crowded with the journalists from the Silver Scout, whispering intently to each other and making phone calls. Hal scanned the crowd.

'Looking for someone?' Mason asked.

'Ryan,' Hal said through gritted teeth. 'He knew this was going to happen, and he did nothing.'

'That's not true,' Hadley said. 'He tried to tell you, didn't he?'

'Maybe that's all he could do,' Mason added.

93

'Where is he?' Hal's eyes re-scanned the crowd. 'I walked through the whole train looking for him, and he's not out here either.'

Uncle Nat had been pulled aside by two police officers. The square-jawed man nodded as a boxy blonde officer talked into her radio and Uncle Nat pointed to Hal. They all walked over.

'Police Sergeant Buckey.' The male officer held out his hand to Hal, who shook it. 'We'd like to ask you some questions.'

'Dad!' Mason called out, as a worried-looking Frank Moretti appeared in the station doorway.

'Chipmunk! Peanut!' Frank ran forward, throwing his arms around his children. 'When they said a girl had been kidnapped . . .' He clutched his heart and shook his head. There were tears in his eyes.

'We're OK, Dad.' Hadley hugged him tight.

'I heard the scream. Everyone on the train rushed to the windows. I ran through the carriages, looking for you.' Frank grabbed his face. 'I thought I saw you, but it wasn't you.' He was babbling now. 'I couldn't find you. I tried to tell an officer. They wouldn't let me off the train, and I thought . . . I thought . . .'

'Dad, I wouldn't let anything happen to Hadley. You know that.' Mason rubbed his dad's arm. 'It was August Reza's daughter that got kidnapped. We saw it.'

'You saw it?' Frank's eyes grew wide. 'Oh, that poor man.'

Uncle Nat offered Frank his hand. 'I'm Nathaniel – Hal's uncle. This is Sergeant Buckey and Officer Bynes from the Omaha Police Department. They want to question

94

the children,' he explained.

'Sure.' Frank Moretti nodded, not letting go of his kids.

'We'll talk to Harrison. Please don't go anywhere,' Officer Bynes said to Hadley and Mason. 'Another officer will take your statements shortly.'

'It's a circus out here,' Sergeant Buckey said. 'We'll go somewhere quiet. Follow me.'

They followed the officers through a side door and into the ticket office, where Hal sat down in a swivel chair. The officers stood with their backs to the counter, the noise of the busy station muted by the glass wall behind them. Sergeant Buckey pulled the blind down.

'Your uncle says you saw an astonishing amount of detail about the kidnapper and their vehicle,' said Officer Bynes, clicking her pen and flipping her notepad open.

'It's all here,' said Hal, taking out his sketchbook.

He repeated everything he'd told his uncle, pointing at his drawing for reference. Officer Bynes scribbled down everything he said, while Sergeant Buckey's narrowed eyes flicked between Hal and the drawing.

'I'm amazed you saw all that,' Sergeant Buckey said, in a disbelieving tone. 'It was kinda dark.'

Hal shrugged. 'The station lights were on.'

'Next you'll be telling us how much the kidnapper weighed,' he joked.

'About eight and a half stone,' Hal replied, 'probably. She's a similar height to my mother, although thinner and, I think, younger.'

95

'So the kidnapper was a woman who weighed 120 pounds?' Sargeant Buckey sounded unconvinced. 'You know her age too?'

'No, but she was strong enough to lift Marianne into the boot, even though she was struggling . . . so I'd guess she's between twenty and thirty.'

'Whoa, kid –' Sergeant Buckey held up his hand – 'these aren't facts.'

'I'm telling you what I saw.' Hal stiffened.

'A drawing isn't evidence,' Officer Bynes said sweetly.

Uncle Nat leaned forward. 'You have the licence plate from Hal, the make and colour of the car?' Officer Bynes nodded. 'If that information can be verified, perhaps you'll consider the rest of Hal's observations?'

'Sure – we'll run a search for the plate immediately.' Officer Bynes flipped her notebook shut.

Hal could tell they weren't taking him seriously.

'Thanks for your help, kid.' Sergeant Buckey winked at Hal. 'We'll take it from here.'

'You're free to return to the train now,' Officer Bynes said, as Sergeant Buckey opened the door.

'Won't the train be cancelled?' Hal said.

Officer Bynes shook her head. 'The crime took place off the train. We're interviewing all witnesses, looking for possible leads. The Reza party will have to remain in Omaha, and we are searching the train now, but there's no need for us to hold up the good, honest people travelling to San Francisco. When we've finished our work, the California Comet will leave.'

96

'What about the Silver Scout?' Uncle Nat asked.

'Once we've finished examining it, it'll stay with the Comet. Mr Reza wants it to take to his home in San Francisco, so it'll be locked up, and then detached in Emeryville.'

Stepping out of the station building, Hal ducked his head at the deafening clatter of helicopter blades. He was momentarily blinded by a dazzling spotlight. He blinked to clear his vision and saw, further up the platform, Officer Bynes walking towards Vanessa Rodriguez. She took something out of the pocket of her leather jacket and showed it to Officer Bynes, then the pair of them walked away talking.

'What are you looking at?' asked Hadley as she came out of the station.

'That woman, Vanessa Rodriguez, she's in the roomette opposite ours. I was wondering why the police would want to talk to her.'

'Maybe she saw something out the window.'

'Whoa, a search copter!' Mason shielded his eyes with his hand. 'Have you seen *Hot Pursuit*? The TV show? The bad guys never get away when there's a search copter on their tail. This is awesome! Marianne will be rescued in no time.'

'I hope they throw the kidnappers in jail,' Hadley said, and Hal nodded.

'Did the police question you?'

'Yeah, a sergeant took our statements,' said Mason.

'I could use a drink,' Frank Moretti said, wiping the sweat from his brow. 'I think the cafe's still open. Do you kids want ice cream? It's great for shock. I know about these things. I'm Italian.'

Hadley and Mason cheered.

'I'd like an ice cream,' Hal said to his uncle. 'Can I go? I couldn't go to sleep now if I tried.'

'Would that be OK with you, Mr Moretti?' Uncle Nat asked.

Mr Moretti nodded. 'I won't let him out of my sight – and please call me Frank.'

'Thank you, Frank.' Uncle Nat smiled sadly at Hal and said in a low voice, 'I am really sorry I let you down. Go and be with your friends. Eat ice cream. I'll be in the roomette if you need me.'

'Working?' Hal said accusingly.

Uncle Nat looked down and nodded. 'The newspapers want the story for tomorrow. It'll be front page news.'

CHAPTER ELEVEN

MOTIVE, MEANS AND OPPORTUNITY

'What do we do now?' Mason said, digging his spoon into a tub of chocolate icc cream.

Hal and his two friends were sitting at the same table they'd sat at with Marianne. Frank was at the counter, talking to Charlie, the cafe attendant, but glancing over at the children every other minute.

'What do you mean?' Hal frowned.

'You're a detective, aren't you?' Mason pointed his spoon at Hal. 'So, let's detect.'

Hal was about to protest that he'd only solved the jewel thief case to save his friend Lenny, but he stopped himself. Marianne was his friend too, wasn't she?

'I'm still freaking out about what you said earlier.' Mason's voice rose in pitch, and he added, in a perfect Crewe accent, '*I feel like I should be able to see something, but I don't know what I'm looking for.*' He slapped the table. 'It's like you could tell this was going to happen.'

Hadley looked at Hal with wide eyes. 'You knew?'

'Not exactly,' Hal said, uncomfortably aware of their unblinking eyes staring at him. 'It's like . . . when you look at a picture and something stands out because it's not what you'd expect to see.' He shook his head. 'Does that make sense?'

Hadley nodded. 'I saw you in the parking lot. You drew everything so fast. You noticed stuff I didn't see, even though we were looking at the same thing.'

'What did the police say about Ryan's message?' Mason asked.

'I didn't tell them,' Hal said, feeling a flash of guilt. 'The police thought my drawing was childish. If I'd told them about Ryan writing an invisible message, it would have sounded silly. They weren't interested in what I had to say.'

'When do adults ever take us seriously?' Hadley tilted her head. 'You should hear the lame jibes I get when I say I'm a magician.' She crossed her arms. 'But we'll have the last laugh.'

'I still can't work out how you made Mason disappear and then reappear in your tiny compartment.'

'Classic misdirection.' Hadley wiggled her fingers. 'Mason hid in the wardrobe. I held your attention while he got in there and used the crystal ball to cover him as he got back out.'

'It's that simple?' Hal looked at Mason with amazement. 'How did I not see?'

'You were looking at what Hadley wanted you to look at. That's magic!' Mason grinned. 'But, what *you* do . . . that's spooky. You had a hunch Marianne was in danger and – *boom!* – she's been kidnapped. Unless you're the kidnapper, you must be one hell of a detective. So, let's crack this thing wide open and work out who's got Marianne.'

'I'm not sure I can. America is so different from back home,' Hal said, pulling out his sketchbook. 'When I solved the jewel thief case, the places, the people and the language were second nature, and my uncle helped me.'

'Yeah, well, this time you have us,' Hadley said.

'At least until Reno, which is the day after tomorrow,' Mason added, 'so we'd better step on it.'

'There are three things we need to work out that will help us decide who the suspects are,' Hal said, flipping over the pages. 'Motive, means and opportunity. The reason for the kidnapping, the way the crime was committed, and what events happened so that the kidnapping could take place.' He stopped at the page where he'd copied down the ransom note. 'Let's start with the motive. Why would anyone want to kidnap Marianne?'

They all looked down.

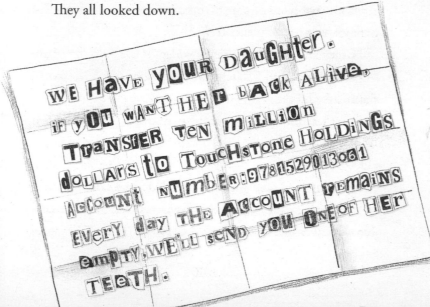

WE HAVE YOUR DAUGHTER.
IF YOU WANT HER BACK ALIVE,
TRANSFER TEN MILLION
DOLLARS TO TouCHSTone HOLDINGS
ACCOUNT NUMBER:9781529013061
EVERY DAY THE ACCOUNT REMAINS
EMPTY, WE'LL SEND YOU ONE OF HER
TEETH.

Hadley winced.

'I can't believe that they only asked for ten million bucks,' Mason said. 'I mean, Reza is one of the richest men in the world. I'd have said fifty or a hundred.'

Hal nodded in agreement. 'The prize for designing Reza's Rocket is a *billion* dollars.'

'Maybe they think Reza's more likely to pay ten million,' Hadley suggested.

'Marianne gave us the motive,' Hal said. 'She told us that people were after her father's money *and secrets.*'

'What secrets?' Hadley asked.

'Business secrets?' Mason suggested.

'The letters in the note were cut from newspaper headlines, like you see in films. So there's no handwriting, and if the kidnappers are clever, there'll be no fingerprints. But we do know one thing . . .' Hal looked at Hadley and Mason. 'It would have taken time to find, cut out and stick all of these letters on to a piece of paper. You can't do it in a hurry. This kidnap was carefully planned.'

Hadley and Mason's eye grew wide.

'What about this Touchstone Holdings bank account?' Mason asked.

'I don't know much about bank accounts, but in movies, baddies have accounts in the Bahamas in false names,' Hadley said.

'I'm sure the police will look into that,' Hal said.

'What about the way the kidnap was done?' Mason said. '*The means!*'

'What do we know?' Hal asked.

'That someone dressed in black, with their face covered, was waiting in that maroon Chevy with the engine running.'

'Yes.' Hal nodded. 'There was only one kidnapper.'

'Everybody knew that August Reza was holding a press conference in Omaha,' Mason said.

'Yes, but not that he was bringing his daughter,' Hal pointed out. 'Which makes the ransom note an important clue.'

'Surely the kidnapper wouldn't have just sat there with the engine running, hoping that Marianne would walk by, on her own, without a bodyguard?' Hadley protested.

'No,' Hal agreed. 'And why did she? Woody goes everywhere with her, and I'd asked Uncle Nat to watch her. Both of them failed.'

Hadley gasped. 'Someone in the Silver Scout is working for the kidnappers! They got Marianne to go outside.'

Hal nodded. 'Away from her bodyguard.'

Mason looked at Hal. 'When we met Marianne, she apologized for hurting you,' he said. 'I gotta know. What did she do?'

'She pulled my hair. We were drawing in her bedroom. I accidentally knocked her pen pots on to the floor. I bent down to pick them up, and she yanked my hair. It really hurt.'

'She pulled your hair?' Hadley looked shocked.

'And screamed at me. She was raging.'

'Whoa.' Mason blinked.

'What did your uncle do?' Hadley asked.

'I didn't tell him,' Hal said. 'He seemed pleased that I was getting along with August Reza's daughter. I didn't want to tell him that she hated me.'

'Did you tell him about the stunt she pulled in her crazy disguise?' Mason asked.

Hal shook his head. 'There wasn't time.' He felt a pang of guilt, knowing that wasn't true. Why hadn't he confided in Uncle Nat?

'Hey, kids – you need to finish up. It's getting late.' Frank pointed to the kiosk attendant, who was pulling down the shutters. 'Charlie here's gonna turn back into a pumpkin if we don't leave soon.'

The train lurched, and they all watched out the window as it crawled out of Omaha station. The spinning red and blue lights on the police cars, the gossiping TV news vans with satellite dishes, and the throng of reporters all slid away – replaced by darkness.

Hal's thoughts turned to Marianne in the boot of that car, and he shivered. Could he have stopped the kidnapping? Where was Marianne now? Was she frightened? He thought about the horrid threat in the ransom note, about her teeth, and he closed his eyes.

'They've the whole state police force looking for her,' Mason said softly. 'And thanks to you, they have the license plate. I'm sure Marianne will be back with her dad by morning.'

'And if she isn't?'

'Then we'll meet at breakfast,' Hadley replied, 'and solve the case ourselves.'

Hal nodded. 'We have to help her.'

Getting up, the three of them followed Frank back to the Morettis' compartment, where they parted ways.

'Night, Sherlock da Vinci,' Mason whispered as he shut their bedroom door.

Hal tiptoed on, becoming aware of the quiet squeaking movements of the carriages and the distant clatter of wheels on rails as they travelled into Nebraska. He carefully slid open the roomette door. His bed had been folded down. Uncle Nat was sat upright in the bottom bunk, fast asleep with his glasses still on and his journal in his lap. Hal gently removed them both, putting them on the shelf and turning off the reading light.

Using the footholds built into the compartment wall, Hal clambered into his bed. Unfolding a blue polyester blanket, which crackled and sparked with static, he stretched out beneath it and closed his eyes. As the carriage rocked him gently, a vision of a terrified Marianne, in her yellow dress, curled up in the boot of a car, forced his eyes open again.

This was not how he'd thought he'd be spending his first night aboard the California Comet.

CHAPTER TWELVE

MOUNTAIN TIME

Hal woke to the smell of coffee and the rumble of the train. The night before, he'd been certain he'd never get to sleep. Lying in his bunk, staring at the ceiling, he'd counted the horn blasts warning stray cattle from the tracks. He remembered counting up to twenty-three, but then he must've dropped off.

'I bring gifts from Francine.' Uncle Nat was standing in the doorway holding a cup of pitch-black coffee in one hand and a bunch of lollipops in the other.

'I'm a bit old for sweets,' Hal said, 'and I don't like coffee.' He was still angry with his uncle for not watching Marianne. He sat up quickly and bumped his head on the ceiling.

'Careful now,' Uncle Nat said softly, as he sat down.

'Is there any news about Marianne?'

'No – but it's early.'

'What time is it?' Hal asked, clambering down and finding that Uncle Nat's bunk was once again two seats.

'Good question,' Uncle Nat replied, with a tentative smile.

'It feels like seven o'clock in the morning, but it's six, because last night we crossed from Nebraska into Colorado and into a new time zone. The clocks went back one hour.' Taking off his chunky silver-strapped watch, he twizzled the silver button on the side. The hands reversed around the navy face as a slender orange hand jerked forward marking the passing seconds.

'I thought that only happened when you went to a different country.'

'America is so big that it has six different time zones. Washington DC in the east and Hawaii in the west are seven hours apart. Last night we left central time, and now we're on mountain time.'

'I don't see mountains.' Hal looked out the window. It was a bright, clear morning. The pale dirt of Colorado stretched as far as the horizon. He'd never thought of America as flat, but he hadn't seen a single hill since Chicago – nearly a thousand miles behind them.

'Today we'll pass through the snow-scattered peaks of the Rockies. The view will be incredible.' Uncle Nat strapped the watch back on. 'If we're lucky, we might spot a bear or a moose.'

Hal pointed at his remaining five watches. 'Don't you need to change the time on those too?'

'The time hasn't changed in Tokyo, or back home.' He held up his right wrist. 'Nor in Berlin, Sydney or Moscow. It is we who are moving, not time.'

Hal shook his head. 'I haven't known what the time is since we landed in America.' He rubbed the sleep from his eyes. 'My body's mixed up about when to eat and when bedtime is.'

'Jet lag can do that to you.' Uncle Nat peered at him with concern. 'Did you manage to get any sleep?'

'A bit.' Hal shrugged. 'I couldn't get Marianne out of my head.'

'Me neither.' Uncle Nat paused, then cleared his throat. 'I'd understand if you didn't want to go over yesterday's drama, but I wonder if we could talk it through?'

'I don't mind.'

'I really am sorry that I let you down,' Uncle Nat said quietly. 'I'd do anything to be able to turn the clock back.'

'What happened?'

'I was in the Silver Scout, on the opposite side of the carriage to Marianne. She was talking to Zola beside the door. Woody was right there next to her. August Reza had demonstrated how his solar battery worked and invited questions from the room. I asked him one and . . . I only took my eyes off Marianne for a minute.' He hung his head. 'Then I saw Woody holding a tray of drinks and realized I couldn't see her. As I crossed the carriage to the door, I heard her scream, and I ran.' He covered his face with his hands and drew in a deep breath, attempting to steady his emotions. He looked at Hal. 'I was too late.'

'I wonder what Marianne and Zola were talking about?'

'Whatever it was, Zola thought it more interesting than August's speech.'

'We should ask her.' Hal looked at Uncle Nat, who nodded in agreement.

'You were on the platform, Hal. You don't think Zola . . . I mean, she wasn't near Marianne?'

'I saw Zola step out of the Silver Scout, alone. Then Marianne screamed . . . I ran . . . I saw her being dragged backwards. Zola was running towards her as hard and fast as I was.'

Uncle Nat looked relieved. 'Hal, you said you thought Marianne was in danger . . . How could you have known?'

'I didn't know Marianne was going to be kidnapped,' Hal said, 'but at Union Station in Chicago, when I was drawing, I got this feeling that something invisible was happening in front of me.' He searched for the right words. 'I saw Marianne cross the concourse with Woody . . .' He fell silent. 'Oh!'

'Yes?' Uncle Nat leaned forward.

'I just remembered something.' Hal reached up to his bunk and grabbed his sketchbook, opening it to the first picture. 'Marianne winked at Ryan. I thought she was being kind because of his head brace. He didn't respond, and I thought he was shy or embarrassed.'

'He is shy, from what I can tell.'

'Yes, but . . .' Hal stared out the window at the scrubland gliding by. 'Do you think they know each other?'

Uncle Nat frowned. 'I can't imagine many scenarios where Ryan Jackson and Marianne Reza would have the opportunity to meet. Didn't you say she went to school in Paris?'

Hal nodded. 'It's weird, but do you remember when we had lunch with Ryan and his dad? Ryan wasn't very talkative, but I got the impression he was trying to tell me something—'

A knock at the door interrupted him, and Uncle Nat reached up to slide it open.

Hadley and Mason were standing in the corridor. 'Morning,' Hadley greeted them.

'Dad's still snoring, but we're hungry,' Mason said.

'And we wondered if there was any news about Marianne?' Hadley added.

'Nothing yet,' Uncle Nat replied.

'You wanna get breakfast with us, Hal?' Mason looked eagerly at him.

Hal gave Uncle Nat a questioning look. 'Can I go?'

Uncle Nat nodded. 'I'll eat with Zola. I have some questions I'd like to ask her.'

'I've got to get dressed,' Hal said to Hadley and Mason. 'Meet you there?'

'Sure thing.' Mason nodded, and the Morettis disappeared.

'Ask Zola if she knows why Marianne went outside, and why Woody wasn't with her,' Hal said, pulling on jeans and a stripy jumper. 'And see if you can find out why Zola went outside too.' He grabbed his socks, stuffed his feet into them, and picked up his shoes. 'See you in the diner.'

'Wait, Hal.' Uncle Nat stood up. 'Are we . . . OK?'

Hal was surprised by the question, realizing his uncle was worried. He nodded. 'We're OK.'

'Thank you,' Uncle Nat replied.

Hal stepped into the corridor and slid the door shut behind him.

'Put those shoes on young man,' Francine called out. 'We

don't want your feet finding anything sharp.'

'Sorry Francine.' Hal crouched down to tie his laces. As he did, he noticed a crumpled sweet wrapper lying on the carpet. He picked it up, examining the purple-and-black foil. Printed in tiny swirling letters were the words *Cassis Réglisse Noire*. He reached into his pocket, and pulled out the sweet Marianne had given him the day before.

They were exactly the same.

CHAPTER THIRTEEN

JULIO'S BREAKFAST

Hal raced to the dining car, following the bitter-sweet scent of coffee, bacon and maple syrup. Earl grinned at him as he rushed in, pointing to the corner table, where Mason and Hadley were waiting.

'Look at this,' Hal demanded, putting the sweet wrapper on the table. 'I found it on the floor outside my roomette.' Mason and Hadley looked bemused. 'These are Marianne's favourites.' He put his sweet beside the wrapper. 'They're French.'

'And?' Hadley asked.

'How did this end up outside my roomette?'

'There are mixed bowls of candy at every coffee station in every carriage,' Mason pointed out. 'I consider it my duty to eat as many of them as I can.'

'Have you eaten any that look like this?' Hal pointed. 'It's blackcurrant liquorice.'

'Ewww, no.'

'So where did it come from?' Hal asked, sitting down. 'These are French. I don't think they're in those bowls.'

112

'But if Marianne was the only person on this train with these sweets,' Hadley said, 'how could that wrapper have ended up outside your roomette?'

'Exactly!' said Hal.

'She could've dropped it yesterday lunchtime, when she was coming through the train trying to escape that Zircona spy,' Mason suggested.

'No. Francine, our carriage attendant, cleans up after everyone all day,' Hal said. 'She'd have swept it up.'

'Then . . .' Hadley shrugged.

'Then –' Hal picked up the wrapper – 'this is a clue!'

'It is?' Mason frowned and stared at it.

'It's a clue. If Marianne *is* the only person on the train with these sweets –' Hal took out his sketchbook and opened it – 'and if it wasn't dropped by her yesterday afternoon –' he placed the wrapper inside and closed it – 'then the fact I found it outside my roomette this morning means something happened last night that we don't know about.'

'But how could Marianne have been on the train last night?' Hadley asked. 'You saw her in the press conference. Your uncle was with her in the Silver Scout, and then we all saw her get kidnapped.'

'I don't know,' Hal admitted.

Earl appeared beside their table. 'What can I get you?'

'I'd like the pancakes,' said Mason.

'Sounds good.' Hadley nodded. 'I'll have pancakes too, please, Earl.'

'And me.' Hal smiled sweetly. 'Hey, Earl, have you seen

Ryan this morning? He's the boy with the braces and the red glasses? We thought he might like to have breakfast with us.'

Mason and Hadley glanced at each other.

Earl shook his head. 'I haven't seen him since yesterday lunchtime.'

'Oh, maybe he's left the train already,' Hal said.

'I doubt it. His father's over there.' Earl pointed to where Gene Jackson was sat with Vanessa Rodriguez and two others, shovelling eggs into his mouth. 'I'll get those pancakes for you right away.' He tucked his pen behind his ear and hurried off.

'Nice detecting!' Hadley looked impressed.

'When I couldn't find Ryan last night, I thought they'd left the train in Omaha.' Hal stared at Gene slurping his coffee. 'But they haven't.' He leaned across the table. 'We need to get Ryan alone and ask him about that message, see if he did know Marianne was going to be kidnapped.'

'We should tell the police about him,' said Hadley.

'We will,' said Hal, 'when we know we're not wasting their time. It could turn out to be nothing.'

'We find Ryan, and we make *him* go to the police.' Hadley nodded.

'Who's on our suspect list?' asked Mason.

'Zola, she was at the scene of the crime, and I think we should find out as much as we can about Seymour Hart,' Hal replied.

'*Zircona spy*,' Mason said in a dramatic movie-trailer voice.

'Good morning, Earl sent me over to join you.' The woman with the blue puffy cloat and beehive of red curly hair lowered her bottom on to the seat beside Hal, squashing him up against the window. 'I hope you don't mind. My name's Adalbert, but you can call me Adie.' Her fuchsia lips parted in a warm smile, a gold tooth nestling among her white ones.

Mason gawped at the iguana draped around her neck. 'Your lizard is so cool!'

'Y'aint 'fraid of lizards, are ye?' Adie said to Hal, using a pirate voice. 'I prefer 'em to parrots.'

'Is he a bearded dragon?' asked Hal.

'Yes!' Adie looked impressed.

'What's its name?' Mason asked.

'Julio,' Adie replied, scratching the lizard's head with the tip of her finger.

'Are lizards allowed on trains in America?' Hal asked.

'Julio gets grouchy when he's cooped up in a travel box.' She made chirruping noises at him and one of his eyes winked. 'No one likes an angry lizard, do they? I'm travelling to Sacramento to stay with my sister. I can't leave him home alone in Chicago – got no one to look after him.

Julio doesn't have a pet passport, so he can't fly. Train's the only way.'

'You're from Chicago?' Mason asked.

Adie nodded. 'That's right.'

Earl arrived with their plates of pancakes and tutted at the sight of Julio. 'Now, Ms Cabbage, we've already had this conversation. Your lizard is not allowed in the dining car.'

Hal glanced at Hadley and Mason, who were trying not to laugh at Adie's surname, and he suppressed a giggle.

'But the children don't mind – do you, kids?'

They all shook their heads.

'If there are complaints, the lizard will have to leave, and you with him,' Earl said, turning away to serve the next table.

Adie rolled her eyes. 'You'd think they'd have more important things to worry about after last night.' She shook her head as she passed Hal the maple syrup. 'Isn't it awful what happened to that Reza girl?'

'Terrible.' Hadley nodded. 'We know her.'

'You *do not*? Oh, honey, that must be tough.'

'She's a friend of Hal's, really,' Mason said.

'It's all anyone is talking about in coach.' Adie stroked Julio's tail. 'They say August Reza and his staff got off the train in Omaha to help the Nebraska police, and that fancy silver carriage of his back there is locked up and empty – that right?'

Hal nodded. 'Yes.'

'Say . . . you weren't the three kids that saw it all happen, were you?'

'Yeah!' Mason beamed. 'Are people talking about us?'

'Why, of course! They're saying how brave you all were.' Adie leaned towards Mason. 'Did you get a good look at the kidnapper?'

'No – they were dressed head to toe in black. Even their face was covered,' Mason said. 'But Hal thinks it was a woman.'

'How can you know that?' Adie asked Hal sharply.

'I don't know for sure,' Hal said. 'It's just that the kidnapper was short.'

'Plenty of short men in the world,' Adie said, looking at Mason and narrowing her eyes. 'Your daddy wouldn't be Frank Moretti, the famous singer? You look a lot like him. I met him in here yesterday afternoon. He's very handsome.'

Mason nodded and blushed. Hadley looked appalled.

'The kidnapper had small feet and a thin waist,' Hal said.

'Oh, I'm sure you got that wrong, dear. I don't think a woman would kidnap that poor girl.' Adie took a matchbox from her coat and looked over her shoulder, winking at Hal before sliding it open and lifting out a struggling cricket by its legs. She offered it to Julio. The lizard's tongue darted out and the cricket was gone. 'Yes, it was obviously a short man.'

Hal felt annoyed that Adie didn't believe him, and he was about to argue when he saw Gene Jackson get to his feet.

'Excuse me, Adie,' Hal said, 'would you let me out? There's something I need to do.'

'OH MY!' exclaimed a diner at the next table. 'Is that a *lizard*?'

Hal squeezed past Adie, accidentally knocking the box of crickets to the floor. He hurried towards Gene, but heard a squeal, followed by cries. He looked back over his shoulder – the dining car had erupted. Crickets were bouncing everywhere and people were shrieking. Some were standing on seats to get away from the bugs; some were on 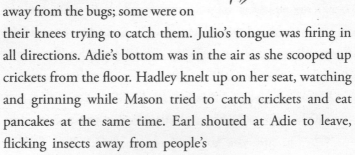 their knees trying to catch them. Julio's tongue was firing in all directions. Adie's bottom was in the air as she scooped up crickets from the floor. Hadley knelt up on her seat, watching and grinning while Mason tried to catch crickets and eat pancakes at the same time. Earl shouted at Adie to leave, flicking insects away from people's food with his dishcloth.

Hal grimaced. He knew he should help, but he didn't want to lose the opportunity to talk to Ryan. He turned, slamming straight into Vanessa Rodriguez, who stood in the aisle transfixed by the action at the other end of the carriage. Apologizing, Hal darted around her. 'Excuse me, Mr Jackson,' he called as Gene disappeared along the corridor. 'Wait!' He ran to catch up, shuffling around an elderly couple, and saw Gene go into the sleeper car. By the time he reached the door, Ryan's dad had gone into his room.

Pausing to catch his breath, Hal knocked. The door opened and Gene looked down at him.

'What do you want?'

'I was wondering if Ryan would like to come to the sightseer lounge with me, to see the Rocky Mountains?'

'Ryan doesn't want to play with you, kid,' Gene replied. 'Go make friends with someone else.'

'Is he OK? I haven't seen him since lunch yesterday and . . .'

Gene looked quizzically at him. 'He's sick. He ate something that didn't agree with him.' Stepping aside, he slid the door open so Hal could see into the compartment. Ryan was sat in the lower bunk reading a comic, a blanket over his legs. 'Hey, Ryan, that British kid is here to see you.'

'Hi!' Hal waved. 'I was wondering if you wanted to come to the sightseer lounge, maybe play cards?'

Ryan shook his head. 'No sank you.' He returned his gaze to the pages of his comic.

'We could hang out later, if you're feeling better,' Hal

said cheerily. 'We could do another *drawing together*, or play *charades*?'

'No sanks,' Ryan lisped, not lifting his eyes from his comic.

'See –' Gene stepped in front of Hal – 'he's sick.'

Thinking of how Francine handled difficult passengers, Hal smiled and said, 'If he wants company, or needs anything, I'm in roomette ten. You have a good day, now.'

Gene grunted and shut the door.

Hal stood still for a moment, listening. He heard Gene say, 'You need to stay away from that kid.' But he couldn't make out Ryan's muffled reply.

CHAPTER FOURTEEN

THE FRENCH DROP

'You missed the fun,' Mason said, as Hal slipped back into his seat in the dining car.

Hadley was lining up silver coins, quarters, on the table. 'Poor Adie and Julio were sent back to coach.' She giggled. 'Earl was *not* happy.'

'Did you see Ryan?' Mason asked.

Hal nodded, fishing a dead cricket from a puddle of maple syrup beside his pancakes. 'He's sick. He was in bed, reading. I thought we'd worked out what his message meant, but now I'm not so sure.'

'But he predicted the kidnapping,' Hadley protested, running her finger along the row of coins.

'Did he?' Hal was uncertain. 'I invited Ryan to come and do some drawing with me and play charades – a coded way of talking about his mimed message –' he shook his head and frowned – 'but I got no reaction. He just went back to reading his comic.'

'That *is* strange.' Hadley looked puzzled.

'When his dad shut the door, I heard him say that Ryan should stay away from me.'

'Maybe Ryan can't talk in front of his dad. That's why he did the miming and drawing,' Mason suggested. 'He might be scared of him.'

'He didn't look scared. He looked . . . fine.'

'I think that makes Gene a suspect too,' Hadley said.

Hal pulled out his sketchbook and drew simple portraits of Seymour Hart, Zola D'Ormond and Gene Jackson.

'Anyone still on this train can't be the person who grabbed Marianne and drove away,' Mason pointed out.

'No, but the kidnapper must have accomplices, and any of these three could have helped.'

Mason nodded. 'We should try Ryan again, when he's on his own.'

'Want to see me make a coin travel through this table?' Hadley asked. 'They say if you stop thinking about a problem, it solves itself.'

'I tried that line with my homework,' said Mason. 'My math teacher was *not* impressed.'

Gene Jackson

'A magic trick sounds good,' said Hal, pushing away his plate of cold pancakes.

'Look.' Hadley picked up a coin. 'I put the coin in this hand.' She closed her fist around it. 'I put my other hand under the table, and – hey presto.' She slammed the hand containing the coin flat

122

on the table, and Hal heard a chiming sound from below it. Hadley flipped her hand palm up. The coin was gone. She pulled her other hand from under the table, and there were two coins in it. 'Would you look at that?' She smiled. 'I doubled my money!'

Mr. Seymour Hart

'That's cool!' Hal was amazed.

'Want me to teach you? Coin tricks are great to learn if you're bored in a hotel room, or on a train, because people always have them in their pockets. That's how I started learning magic. We were in a casino hotel in Atlantic City, Pop was working, and this nice bellhop taught me a coin trick. I practised it, and then I learned another and another.'

'Show me.' Hal nodded, picking up a quarter.

'Put your left hand out flat so the audience can see it. That's it. Place the coin on the palm of your hand and withdraw your other hand. Good. Now, you're going to turn your left hand over . . . Wait – not yet. As you begin to turn it, pull your elbow back so your hand is over your lap. As you turn your hand, make a fist around the coin. Do it. Good. Now go back to the open-hand position. This time, when you turn your hand over, let the coin drop into your lap as you make the fist.

Zola D'Ormond

The audience won't see it, especially if you keep looking at your fist.'

'Adie lied to us,' Mason said, as Hal practised letting the coin drop into his lap.

'What about?' Hal asked, as the coin slid from his hand and clattered on to the table.

'She said she was from Chicago, but she's not. She's putting on an accent. I think she's originally from Boston.'

'What has that got to do with anything?' Hadley gave him a withering look, then returned her attention to Hal. 'Next, you tell the audience you're putting your other hand under the table to catch the coin. As you do it, you pick up the coin in your lap. I had a spare one down there, so I picked both up – it helps with the jangle noise. Here – put this one in your lap and try it.'

Hal laughed at how simple it was and performed the trick for Hadley.

'Perfect!' Hadley nodded encouragingly. 'In magic, the handling of objects is called *palming*.' She picked up a quarter with her left hand, grabbed it with her right, whispered '*Abracadabra*', and then flicked her fist open. The coin was gone. She reached over and pulled it out from behind Hal's ear.

Hal picked up another coin and tried to make it look like he was putting it into his right hand while palming it in his left, but it fell on to the table with a clang, and Mason laughed.

'You need to learn the French Drop,' Hadley said. 'That's this move.' She turned her hands so he could see the action of how she let a coin drop into her cupped fingers, while pretending to grab it with her other fist. 'It's one of the principal moves of magic. I practise it every day. You can do it with rolled-up balls of paper; or small fruits, like grapes; or coins.' She performed it again, and even though Hal knew she'd palmed the coin, he still somehow felt it must be in her closed fist. 'All magic is misdirection. The performance is everything.'

Hidden coin

There was a gentle lurch as the train came to a standstill in the middle of a knotted mess of track. Mason looked out the window. 'We're going backwards.'

'Denver is a terminus – they reverse us in,' said Hal.

Hadley and Mason looked at him.

Hidden coin

'What? I looked it up before I came. We stop in Denver for at least half an hour for maintenance checks before the train heads into the Rockies. I like trains, OK?'

'Such a nerd.' Mason grinned. 'A British nerd.'

The platforms of Denver station slid into view, and the train came to a halt.

Hidden coin

'Look,' Hadley said, tapping the window. 'Seymour Hart's just got out. So he didn't leave the train in Omaha.'

'He's got his briefcase,' Hal said. 'Looks like he's in a hurry.'

'Let's follow him,' said Mason, scrambling to his feet. 'Isn't that what detectives do?'

As they rushed through the dining car, they passed Uncle Nat having breakfast with Zola. She was clutching her coffee cup with both hands and looked shaken.

'We're going to stretch our legs,' Hal said as they ran past.

'We're only stopping for half an hour!' Uncle Nat called after him.

As Hal jumped off the train, he looked up at the impressive white roof encircling the platforms like a slow-cresting wave. He thought about drawing it until Mason hissed, 'There he is!'

Seymour Hart was walking briskly across a concrete-and-glass footbridge that spanned the platforms.

Pushing against a tide of passengers, the three of them dashed after their suspect, following him along the concourse and into the station: a grand foyer with high windows and glittering chandeliers.

Glancing up at the station clock, Seymour hurried towards the staircase.

'C'mon, guys!' Mason hissed, scurrying after him.

At the top of the stairs they saw an elegant bar of marble and polished brass, with a view of the foyer below. Lit by a shaft of sunlight, Seymour sat on a leather stool beside a tall man in a smart jacket. Hal put his sketchbook on the floor and quickly drew the scene.

126

'What's he doing?' Hadley whispered.

Opening his briefcase, Seymour Hart turned it towards his companion. The other man's face lit up as he peered inside. Lifting a black box from the case, Seymour held it out. The man slid an envelope across the bar and took the box. Opening the envelope, Seymour pulled out a wad of dollar bills and counted them. Nodding, he put the envelope into the briefcase, closed and locked it. After shaking hands, the other man put the box in his pocket, got up, and began to

walk directly towards Hal and his friends, who were kneeling on the stairs.

'Quick – run!' hissed Hadley, and all three of them turned and sprinted down the stairs, out of the main door and into the car park at the front of the station.

'That looked super shady!' gasped Mason, stopping to catch his breath.

Hal nodded, panting hard. 'We need to find out what was in that box.'

CHAPTER FIFTEEN

THE UNBELIEVABLE TOOTH

Hadley pointed at a line of red and yellow metal boxes that dispensed newspapers. 'Look! Maybe there's news about the kidnapping.'

'They might have found Marianne,' said Mason, sounding hopeful.

Hadley dropped four quarters from her pocket into the slot of one of the boxes and yanked open the hatch, pulling out a paper. A photograph of Marianne's face filled the front page. 'They haven't found her,' she said, as they crowded around her to read.

Thirteen-year-old Marianne Reza, daughter of tech billionaire August Reza and UN ambassador Camille Brodeur, was kidnapped last night from Omaha station. The kidnapper, dressed in black with their face obscured, left a ransom note demanding money for her safe return.

Concerns for Marianne Reza's safety escalated when a tooth was delivered to her father's home in San Francisco in the early hours of this morning. DNA tests confirm it belongs to the kidnapped girl.

A maroon Chevrolet used for the abduction was a hire car. It was found abandoned a few streets away from the station, leaving the police with no significant leads in the case.

Hadley had gone deathly pale. 'They pulled out her tooth like the ransom note said . . . I didn't think they'd actually do that.'

'. . . *a few streets away*,' Hal muttered, looking up at the facade of the station where a neon sign said *Union Station – Travel by Train*. 'Urgh! None of this makes sense!' He felt sick.

'They must have had a second car waiting,' Mason said. 'They switched cars. That's why the police didn't catch them.'

'I need to think,' Hal snapped, turning away and walking back into the station. His heart was banging on his ribs as if it was trying to break out. He felt tears pricking the backs of his eyes. He clenched his fists, suddenly furious again at his uncle for not watching Marianne like he'd promised. As he climbed the stairs to the footbridge, clues swirled about his mind, taunting him.

Mason and Hadley hurried after him.

Hal pulled out his sketchbook, leaned it against the railing in the middle of the bridge, and lightly marked perspective lines on a clean page. 'Who would want to kidnap Marianne Reza?' His pencil darted across the paper, furiously outlining the stone edifice of the old station in front of him. 'If it's Zircona, it's not for ten million dollars, is it? That's not a lot of money to Reza or to them. Are they after the secrets to Reza's inventions? Perhaps . . .' He drew the arc of the stadium-like roof. 'But if that's what they're after . . . If that's what they're after . . .' He cleared his throat and blinked back his tears, concentrating on marking in the station clock. 'Then they don't need to pull out her teeth.'

'You OK?' Hadley asked softly.

'I can't get that sweet wrapper out of my head,' he replied. 'It means something. I know it.'

'When we get back on the train, we'll check the sweet bowls,' Mason said.

Hal stared down at the California Comet, drawing the

snaking carriages. Two workers in blue Amtrak uniforms were unloading boxes of food and supplies from a trolley. Three in yellow hard hats wiped suds from the windows of the sightseer lounge with a long mop. Seconds later they appeared in his picture.

'They're cleaning the windows cos the Rockies are coming up,' Hadley said quietly. 'The view is out of this world.'

Hal expanded his sketch to the platform. Adalbert Cabbage was sitting on a bench with Julio on her lap. Vanessa Rodriguez stood at the far end of the platform, glaring at the lizard. Hal wondered again why Officer Buckey had been talking to her in Omaha.

'There's Ryan's dad.' Hadley pointed out Gene Jackson hurrying along the platform. He had a duffel bag slung over his shoulder. 'He's in a hurry.'

Gene Jackson appeared in the drawing.

'Is it like a computer inside your head right now?' Mason asked. 'Except instead of zeros and ones, you have pictures fitting together like jigsaw pieces? Is that how the detecting thing works?'

'Right now, my mind is completely blank,' Hal muttered.

'Seymour Hart's getting back on the train.' Hadley pointed.

'What is that man up to?' Mason asked.

'Look –' Hadley leaned over the railing – 'you can see down into the Silver Scout from up here.' They all peered over the bridge and through the glass roof of August Reza's observation dome. It was possible to make out the murky shapes of his bedroom furniture. 'I wonder if my hoodie is in there somewhere.'

'It'll be in Marianne's bedroom,' Hal replied. 'That's round the other side.'

'I know it's not important, compared to what's happened to Marianne, but I'm sad about losing that hoodie. Dad had it made specially for my birthday. I don't want to have to tell him I lost it.'

'I wish we could have a look inside,' Mason said, resting his head on his hands. 'There might be a clue in there.'

'It's locked,' Hal said. 'There's a key code to get in.'

'We could try to work it out,' Hadley suggested. 'It may be something simple like zero zero zero.'

'I don't think August Reza would have zero zero zero as his door code,' Mason scoffed. 'He's a genius.'

'Well, then, maybe it's the Fibonacci Sequence,' said Hadley, 'or a famous number like pi – *three point one four one five nine* – oh, except that goes on for infinity . . .'

Hal pointed his pencil at Frank Moretti, who was yawning and stretching as he stepped off the train. 'Look, there's your dad.'

'Anytime Pop needs a number, he uses Elvis's birthday,' said Mason. 'It's the code for his cell phone, for his bank card – everything.'

'He's looking for us,' Hadley said, watching her father amble up the platform. She lifted her hand and waved. 'Pop!'

Frank Moretti spotted them and waved back. Hadley and Mason ran down the stairs to meet him.

Hal closed his sketchbook, and was about to follow them, when he glimpsed movement in the master bedroom of the Silver Scout. He leaned out over the railings, his whistle dangling from his neck. He studied the dome but saw nothing more through the glass. He frowned. There shouldn't be anyone in there. He wished he knew the code to the door. Closing his eyes, he pictured Marianne's fingers on the keypad. He saw her index finger press the first button.

It was the number seven.

CHAPTER SIXTEEN

THE CANDIED CLUE

Hal caught up with Hadley and Mason, who were busily reassuring their dad that they were safe.

'We should get back on the train,' Mason said.

'Let's look in the bowls of sweets,' Hal suggested, as they climbed aboard.

'I want to know what Seymour Hart keeps in his briefcase,' Hadley said. 'I keep thinking about that box he handed over for money. What if one of Marianne's teeth was inside?'

Mason tutted. 'If he were an evil dentist working for the kidnappers, he wouldn't be on this train, would he? He'd be wherever Marianne is.'

'Let's focus on that sweet wrapper,' Hal said, heading towards his roomette.

Mason paused at the coffee station and emptied the bowl of mixed candy into his pockets. He unwrapped a Jolly Rancher lollipop and put it in his mouth.

'I want to test something,' Hal said. 'Drop the wrapper on the floor outside my roomette.'

Mason let the wrapper fall to the floor as he followed Hadley and Hal into the roomette and perched on the arm of Hal's chair.

'No blackcurrant liquorice in the bowl,' he said, emptying his pockets on to the seat.

The Comet's horn blasted, echoing around the station. The doors hissed shut and the train pulled out of Denver.

'Someone's left you a note,' Hadley said, passing Hal a folded piece of paper with his name on it.

Opening it, Hal recognized Uncle Nat's neat looping handwriting.

Hal, I'm in the sightseer lounge. This leg of the journey has spectacular views and is the reason 1 wanted to bring you on the California Comet. So, bring your sketchbook. I'm saving you a seat.
Uncle Nat

Hal pulled a face.

'What is it?' Hadley asked.

'Uncle Nat wants me to go to the sightseer lounge and look at the view.'

'You should,' Mason said. 'The Rockies are cool.'

'I know. I mean, I want to, but staring at mountains isn't going to help Marianne, is it? In twenty-four hours, she'll lose another tooth.'

'. . . And me and Mason have to get off the train,' Hadley added.

'So, we separate,' Mason said. 'Doesn't mean we stop investigating.'

'That's true.' Hal perked up. 'Uncle Nat might have found out something from his breakfast with Zola – like what she was doing outside the Silver Scout.'

'I'm going to work out a way to see inside Seymour Hart's briefcase,' Hadley said.

'Francine!' Hal waved as the carriage attendant shuffled past the door backwards with a dustpan and brush in her hands. Mason's lollipop wrapper was in the tray.

'Well, hello.' She straightened up and smiled. 'You children having a good time?'

They all nodded.

'Hal's challenged me to eat all the complimentary candy in the dish.' Mason held up a fistful of sweets.

'Don't you go making yourself sick,' she said, her eyes twinkling.

'I won't.' Mason grinned. 'Say, have you got any of the blackcurrant liquorice candy? With the purple-and-black wrapper? You know, the ones with the fancy French name?'

Francine looked blankly back at him and shook her head.

'These,' Hal said, pulling Marianne's sweet from his trouser pocket.

'I'm sorry, sugar. I ain't seen candy like that before – certainly not on Amtrak.'

'Francine –' Hadley smiled sweetly – 'I lost an earring last night in the corridor outside this roomette. You haven't found it, have you?'

'No dear, I haven't.'

'We saw you sweeping,' Hadley continued, 'and wondered if anyone cleans the corridor at night. Maybe they found it?'

Francine shook her head. 'It's just me that takes care of the sleeping cars on this train. I clean during the day, from around six in the morning, when it's light and the sound doesn't bother folks. I stop when dinner is served, at six.'

Hal jumped to his feet. 'Thank you, Francine. You've been really, really helpful.'

'Glad to be of service,' she replied, looking baffled by Hal's gratitude, and returning to sweeping the corridor.

'I was right!' Hal felt exhilarated.

'Yeah – but what does it mean?' Mason sucked hard on his lollipop.

'It means the sweet wrapper was dropped in this corridor between six o'clock last night and six o'clock this morning. And as Marianne is the only person on this train with these sweets –' he held it up – 'she must have been here too.'

'Unless, by some crazy coincidence, there's a French

138

passenger on this train who likes *Cassis Réglisse Noire*,' Hadley pointed out.

'Which is unlikely,' Hal replied.

'Marianne was kidnapped at 7.30 p.m.,' Mason said.

'Yes.' Hal felt a surge of excitement. 'And why haven't the police picked up any leads on where Marianne is?'

'Because the kidnappers switched cars,' Mason said.

'Or . . . what if the kidnapper drove around the corner, abandoned the car, and returned to the train after the police had searched it?' Hal clenched his fist around the sweet, looking from Mason to Hadley. 'Marianne could be on this train.'

There was a moment of dumbstruck silence.

'I don't want to burst your bubble, Hal,' Hadley said, biting her lip, 'but how would the kidnapper have sent that tooth to August Reza if they were on the train?'

Mason nodded. 'And if they pulled out her tooth here, it'd have been . . . noisy.' He winced. 'Someone would have heard something.'

'Not if she's in the Silver Scout,' Hal said.

Hadley sat up straight. 'But you said it was empty.'

'It was empty when the train left Omaha. We don't know if it's empty now.' He looked from Hadley to Mason. 'Think about it. Where is the one place on this train that no one can get into?'

Mason stood up. 'You really think Marianne could be in the Silver Scout?'

'It's possible. The kidnappers could have brought Marianne

on to the train after the police had searched it and hidden her in a roomette. The sweet wrapper must have fallen from her pocket, or . . .' He stopped. 'Perhaps she dropped it on purpose.'

'Like a message?' Hadley said.

'Maybe.' Hal's first thought, when he'd found the sweet wrapper, had been that Marianne had dropped it hoping he would find it, even though he knew she didn't know which roomette was his. 'What if the kidnappers then took Marianne off the train, in the middle of the night, at a station down the line from Omaha – McCook, say – and carried her to the Silver Scout?'

'They'd have to know the door code,' Hadley pointed out.

'Marianne knows it,' Mason said.

'Guys, this is crazy.' Hadley looked alarmed.

'But it's *possible*,' Hal said. 'And there's something else. When we were leaning over the footbridge in Denver I thought I saw someone moving about in August Reza's bedroom. What if they're still there?'

CHAPTER SEVENTEEN

ROCKY RAILROAD

'There you are.' Uncle Nat was sat in the middle of a two-seater sofa at the centre of the sightseer lounge, a book about American railways open on his lap. 'I'd begun to worry you'd been left behind in Denver.'

Hal smiled. 'I was with Mason and Hadley.'

'I'm glad you've made friends.' Uncle Nat moved up so Hal could sit down.

'Did you read the paper?' Hal said. 'They sent one of Marianne's teeth to her dad.'

'You saw that?' Uncle Nat sighed. 'I was hoping you hadn't.'

From their sofa they had a panoramic view of the passing landscape. Crowding in from the rest of the train, passengers filled the seats and were standing in the aisle, testing their cameras and flicking through their guidebooks.

'Let's try to enjoy this bit of the journey.' Uncle Nat forced a smile. 'The scenery is otherworldly.'

'I don't understand why Mr Reza doesn't just pay the ransom and get Marianne back,' Hal blurted out, unable to help himself. 'That's what I would do, and he can afford it.'

'It's not that simple,' Uncle Nat said, lowering his voice. 'If August pays the money, there's nothing to stop the kidnappers refusing to give Marianne back and asking for more. Or, even worse, they take the money *and* Marianne and disappear. The police use ransom negotiations to try to work out who they're dealing with, and where the kidnappers are keeping their victim. They'll have told August not to pay the ransom.' He clasped his hands together. 'Now, please, let's not talk about this any more. It's upsetting.'

Hal turned to look out the window as the California Comet rattled away from the office blocks and highways of Denver, rising on a great curving track cutting into the side of a hill. He pointed to a line of rusting containers in the distance. 'What are those?'

'Coal cars filled with rocks and rubble – otherwise known as hoppers.' Uncle Nat pushed his glasses up his nose. 'They serve as a windbreak to protect the trains as they go around this curved bit of track – it's known as the Big Ten. Wind speeds can reach one hundred miles an hour as they sweep down the mountains into the valley. About forty years ago, a freight train was blown right off the tracks. That's when they put the hoppers there.'

Hal pulled out his sketchbook and drew the curved track, with the coal cars above it in the near distance, plants sprouting out of the rubble-filled trucks. The train was going slower now, carefully handling the tight curves, threading through pine trees and outcrops of rock, and always climbing.

'I spoke to Zola about Marianne,' Uncle Nat said suddenly. 'She's terribly shaken by what happened. She said that Marianne had approached her in the Silver Scout while August Reza was talking about his new batteries. Marianne said that she had something top secret to tell Zola about her father's competition. Zola asked her what it was, but Marianne said she couldn't talk with so many people around. She suggested they go outside, and Zola agreed. Marianne sent Woody off to get her a drink and slipped outside first, telling Zola to wait for a minute and then follow her.'

'What did Marianne want to tell Zola?'

'Zola never found out. When she stepped outside, she heard Marianne scream and saw exactly what you saw – the kidnapper grab Marianne, drag her back to the car, and throw her in the boot.'

The verdant canopy of firs and pines thinned and parted, offering a glimpse of Colorado. The state stretched out below them like a living map, criss-crossed by highways and factories puffing smoke. The lounge erupted with gasps, and chatter, and cameras clicked.

Hal looked up at his uncle. 'Do you believe Zola?'

Uncle Nat hesitated. 'I want to believe her. She seemed to be telling the truth.'

'Because it would make more sense if the story was the other way around. If Zola had persuaded Marianne to go outside . . .'

'I know –' Uncle Nat pursed his lips – 'but Zola wouldn't get mixed up in a kidnapping. She's built a formidable career on exposing criminals. That takes hard work and guts. To then become one?'

'But how could the kidnappers have known that Marianne would come out of the Silver Scout? Woody follows her everywhere. She shouldn't have been standing out there on her own. No one could have known she would be.'

'Indeed.' Uncle Nat stared out the window. 'It's puzzling.'

The carriage was plunged into darkness. The emergency exit signs around the windows glowed green as passengers exclaimed excitedly to each other.

'We've entered the tunnel district,' Uncle Nat explained to Hal. 'Twenty-eight of them cut right through the Rocky Mountains, and some are extraordinarily long.'

Sunlight drenched the carriage as they emerged from the tunnel, and Hal saw that a man two seats along was reading a newspaper. It was different from the paper he'd looked at with Hadley and Mason, but it too had a picture of Marianne on the front.

It was an old photograph – she was younger. There were balloons behind her, and a cake with candles. Staring at the image, his eyes lost focus, and he felt two thoughts merge. He flicked through the pages of his sketchbook, and finding what he was looking for, jumped to his feet.

'Are you all right?' Uncle Nat asked.

'Err, yes, I've just remembered, I promised Hadley and Mason that I'd . . . help them with their magic act,' Hal babbled. 'I need to go.'

The carriage went dark again, and Hal stood still, waiting. Two minutes later, blinded by a flood of sunlight, he found himself standing nose to nose with Vanessa Rodriguez. Surprised, he stepped backwards, falling back into his seat.

'Hi,' she said, with no trace of warmth.

'Hello –' Uncle Nat replied – 'Ms Rodriguez, isn't it? Would you like a seat? Hal was just leaving.'

'I want to ask you some questions.' Her voice was monotone.

'Sure.' Uncle Nat nodded. 'How can I help you?'

'Not you –' she looked at Hal – 'him.' Hal looked at his uncle. 'You had breakfast this morning with the woman who released the crickets in the dining car.'

'That was my fault.' Hal wondered if he was in trouble.

'That was *you*?' Uncle Nat suppressed a smile.

'I accidentally knocked her box of crickets over. Adie was giving Julio his breakfast.'

'Julio?' Vanessa frowned.

'Her pet bearded dragon.'

'Right. What did you say her name was?'

'Adie – her full name is Adalbert Cabbage.'

Vanessa snorted and looked away.

'Do you know her?' Uncle Nat asked Vanessa, and she nodded as the train dived into another tunnel. The passengers' whoops and chatter were getting louder with each tunnel they went through. The light returned.

'What did you talk about with . . . Adalbert Cabbage?' Vanessa asked.

'Err . . . her lizard and whether we minded her having him at the table, which we didn't. Then she started feeding him, and that's how I came to knock over the crickets.'

'I don't care about the bouncing bugs, kid. Did she talk about anything else?'

Hal bristled. 'We talked about the kidnapping. She wanted to know what we'd seen.'

'I'm sorry,' Uncle Nat interjected, 'but has Hal upset you in some way?'

'Apology accepted,' Vanessa replied, silencing him, 'and no, the kid has not upset me.' She fixed Hal with an intense stare. 'What did Adalbert say, *exactly*?'

'She asked if the Silver Scout was locked up and empty and said how awful it was that we'd witnessed the kidnapping. She asked what we'd seen, so I told her I thought the kidnapper was a woman, and she . . .'

'You think the kidnapper is a woman?' Vanessa's eyebrows rose. 'Why?'

'Her height, the size of her feet, and the fact she had a waist and hips,' Hal replied, tired of having to justify his observation to people who didn't believe him.

'Interesting.' Vanessa nodded. 'What did Ms Cabbage say to that?'

'She thought I'd got it wrong and that the kidnapper must have been a short man.'

'Who on earth is Adalbert Cabbage?' Uncle Nat asked.

'Someone you should avoid,' Vanessa replied. She looked at Hal. 'I mean it. Don't talk to her again.'

'Why not?'

'Does Adalbert Cabbage sound like a real name to you?' Vanessa asked, her top lip curling into a half-smile. 'Anyone using a phoney name has dishonourable intentions. If I were you, I'd give Adalbert Cabbage and her lizard a wide berth.'

Everyone in the carriage *ooooo*ed as the train entered another tunnel. When they came out the other side, Vanessa Rodriguez was gone.

CHAPTER EIGHTEEN

WINTER PARK

'Can't let you through, buddy,' said a man wearing an Amtrak uniform. 'No passing between carriages while we're in a tunnel. You'll let in diesel fumes. Makes everyone sick.'

Hal stared through the glass into the dining car and let out a little yelp as he spotted Ryan in a red T-shirt sitting at a table. The tunnel seemed to go on forever. He watched as Ryan got up and followed Genc to the dining-car door.

Sunlight blazed in through the windows once again, and Hal slammed his hand on the metal plate to slide the door open.

'Ryan!' he called out, dashing down the aisle between the dining booths. The train slipped again into darkness. 'Oh, come *on*.' Hal stood by the next door, staring at the blacked-out windows, willing the train to come out of the tunnel.

'Isn't this a thrill,' said an old lady who was sat in a booth, her arm linked through her husband's. His eyes twinkled as he smiled back at her.

Daylight returned, and Hal hurried into the sleeper carriage. Francine was in the corridor, carrying a pile of linen. 'Have you seen Ryan Jackson?' Hal asked her.

'The kid with the braces?' she said. 'Sure – he went downstairs. Looked in a hurry.'

Hal clattered down the stairs into the vestibule. He saw a changing room, showers, and the branches of pine trees scraping the window of the exit door. 'Ryan?' He called out.

A toilet door opened an inch.

'Rot do you ront?' Ryan lisped.

'Are you OK?' Hal asked. He could see one of Ryan's eyes and some of his metal face scaffolding through the gap.

'No.' Ryan looked down. 'Got yellyache.'

'What?'

'*Yellyache!*' Ryan repeated, clutching his stomach and glaring at Hal.

'I need to ask you about Marianne.'

'Who?' Ryan let out a low groan.

'The girl who was kidnapped.'

'What arout her?'

'Do you know her?'

'No.' Ryan shook his head. 'Rot rakes you sink I do?'

'Your message . . .' Hal faltered. 'You mimed her name.' It sounded ridiculous now he was saying it out loud. 'You scored the page in my sketchbook.'

'No I ridn't.' Ryan shook his head and groaned. 'I gotta go.' He shut the door and locked it.

Hal stepped back, reeling as the train slipped into another

tunnel and luminous paint lit up the staircase in eerie green. He'd got it all wrong! How could he have mistaken Ryan's actions so completely? He blinked as sunlight lasered back in through the window.

'Hal? Are you down there?' Mason's face appeared at the top of the stairs, and he beckoned to him. 'We've had an idea.'

'Idea?' Hal followed Mason through to the next sleeper car. 'Idea about what?'

'How to find out what's in Seymour's briefcase.' Mason grinned and led Hal downstairs to where Hadley was waiting for them in the next vestibule. The train sounded its horn and birds fluttered up from the treetops.

'*Another* tunnel!' Mason exclaimed.

'This is the long one before Fraser,' Hadley said, as the light in the carriage dimmed.

'The Moffat Tunnel,' Hal said. 'It's six miles long. Right now, there's half a mile of rock above our heads.'

'Dude!' Mason shook his head. 'How d'you know this stuff?'

'Books,' Hal replied, sitting down, cross-legged, on the floor. 'Listen, I have news.'

Mason and Hadley sat down either side of him and he told them what Uncle Nat had said about Zola.

'She's got to be lying,' Hadley said.

The floor rumbled beneath them as the train pressed on through the dark.

'Uncle Nat thinks she's telling the truth.' Hal shrugged. 'He's known her for ages. But that's not all . . .' And he relayed

his conversation with Vanessa Rodriguez.

'What?' Mason leaned back. 'Adie's not dangerous.'

'We don't know that,' Hadley said. 'She does have a weird name, and you said she was lying about where she was from.'

'You were listening to me?' Mason was surprised.

Hadley shrugged. 'I do sometimes, ya know.'

'We should add Adie to our suspect list,' Hal said.

'We should also add Vanessa Rodriguez,' Mason said. 'Did you see the police questioning her in Omaha?'

'I did.' Hal nodded. 'She's strange. Talking to her is like being interrogated by a supervillain.' It grew brighter. 'We're pulling into Fraser.' He got up and looked out the window.

A speaker above their head crackled. '*There will be a fifteen-minute stop here at Fraser so that those going to the Winter Park ski resort can retrieve their luggage.*'

Hal turned to Mason and Hadley. 'There's something I need to do, right now.'

'What is it?'

'Follow me,' said Hal.

It was freezing cold on the platform. The horizon was a shark's mouth of mountain peaks. An icy wind stole the breath from Hal's throat, and he wished that he'd thought to grab his anorak. Mason didn't seem to notice the cold, but Hadley was huddled against her big brother for warmth.

'We're nine thousand feet above sea level, according to Uncle Nat.' Hal shivered, quickening his pace. 'This station is the highest point on the Amtrak network.' He looked at Mason. 'It's all downhill from here.'

Mason shook his head. 'You should leave the jokes to me.'

'What are we doing out here?' Hadley's teeth were chattering. 'Other than t-turning into icicles.'

'Remember how you said people pick memorable numbers as codes?' Hal said. 'Well, I think I know the number that will open that door.' He pointed to the Silver Scout.

'Hal.' Hadley stopped. 'You can't!' She looked over her shoulder.

'Relax. Look, I'm not even certain I know the door code,' Hal said, gritting his teeth to stop them chattering, 'but I've got to try.'

'What if the kidnappers are inside?' Mason said as they neared the door. 'What will you do?'

'Let's see if this works first.' Hal's heart hammered in his chest as he flipped open the cover to the keypad. His fingers were cold and clumsy, but he swallowed and typed *70707* on the cold metal buttons. It was the number he'd seen on August Reza's model train. The number he'd drawn in his sketchbook. And, he guessed, Marianne's birthday. He heard a *clunk*. He reached for the handle of the door – and it opened.

'No way,' Mason whispered.

Hal stepped up into the private railcar.

'What are you *doing*?' Hadley hissed.

'Wait here,' Hal replied. 'If you hear me cry out, run and get help.'

'No, Hal!' Mason stepped towards him.

'If Marianne is here, then this ends now.' And with that, Hal turned and headed into the white corridor of the Silver Scout.

CHAPTER NINETEEN

SCOUTING
FOR SECRETS

As he crept along the corridor into the Silver Scout, Hal's shallow breaths and booming heartbeat screamed to his brain that this was a stupid idea. He pushed open the first door – an empty roomette with seats of white leather. August Reza had called it the staff bedroom. He guessed it was where Woody slept.

There was a noise behind him. Hal opened his mouth to yell, then saw Mason's bulging eyes peeping around the corner.

'*What are you doing?*' Hal mouthed.

'Can't let you do this on your own,' Mason whispered. 'Hadley's by the door. We'll yell like crazy if we see anyone. She'll run and get help.'

Hal nodded, immediately feeling better with Mason beside him. He slid open the door to Marianne's room and gasped. Drawers and cupboards were open; clothes and books were strewn everywhere. The pots of pens she'd arranged so carefully were now lying empty on the bed, their contents scattered

across the mattress. The pink flamingo duvet was balled up on the floor.

Mason leaped forward with his fists raised. 'There's no one here.'

'Look at this mess,' Hal said. 'This place has been ransacked!'

Mason raised an eyebrow. 'You should see my bedroom.'

'Marianne would freak out if she saw her room like this.' Hal thought about how she'd reacted when he'd knocked over her pens. Had that only been yesterday morning?

'C'mon.' Mason waved him on, and they tiptoed down the corridor side by side.

They passed an empty kitchen, and Mason poked his head round the doorway to the meeting room.

'Whoa . . .'

'What is it?'

'This place is classy.'

Hal shoved him through the room. 'Don't touch anything,' he hissed. 'We don't want to get into trouble. Come on – this way.' He crept into the viewing lounge. 'There's no one here,' he said, with a mixture of relief and disappointment. 'Wait – check upstairs.'

Mason disappeared up the stairs to Reza's bedroom, and a minute later, poked his head back down. 'Nada, zip, nothing, zilch.'

'Did you check the bathroom?'

'Yup.'

Hal's shoulders, which had been up by his ears, dropped, and he had to admit to himself that he was wrong again. Nobody was using the Silver Scout as a hideout. 'OK. I'll go and get Hadley.'

Hal sped back through the carriage to where Hadley was waiting, looking terrified. 'It's OK,' he said. 'There's no one here.'

'Let's go then,' Hadley said, beckoning him to come. 'People are getting back on the train. Where's Mason?'

They heard a whistle, signalling the train was ready to leave.

'Let's ride to Granby in the Silver Scout.'

'Hal!' Hadley looked scandalized.

'We need to search for clues. Marianne's bedroom has been turned over and I want to draw it.'

'Her bedroom's been turned over?'

'Sis, get in,' Mason called over Hal's shoulder. 'You can look for your Houdini hoodie.'

'Good idea!' Hadley scrambled into the Silver Scout

joining Hal and her brother.

Hal closed the door and they all felt the carriage shift as they pulled out of Fraser station. The three of them looked at each other, electrified by the sensation of doing something forbidden.

'We're here to help Marianne,' Hal said, more to reassure himself than the Morettis. 'We're looking for clues.'

'And my hoodie,' Hadley added.

'Come on then, Sherlock da Vinci,' said Mason. 'What should we do first?'

'Split up. Mason, you search the upstairs bedroom. Hadley, you take the viewing lounge and meeting room. Look for anything that seems out of place. I'm going to draw Marianne's bedroom.' He looked at Hadley. 'When I've finished, you can hunt for your hoodie.'

'I can't believe this place doesn't have a TV,' Mason said.

'It does,' Hal replied. 'Go into the meeting room and say, *Screen on.*' He watched Mason walk away and waited.

'NO WAY! Hadley, come and check out the size of this thing!' Mason called out. 'It's bigger than that one in Atlantic City.'

Hal grinned as Hadley ran to see. Taking out his sketchbook, he sank to the floor in the doorway of Marianne's bedroom. Her window framed views of distant ski chalets and close-up tufts of mountain grass wearing cloaks of snow. Trying not to think too hard, Hal drew what he could see in the ransacked bedroom. He thought about the negative space in his picture, the parts he was leaving blank. He tried to notice not only what was in front of him, but also what he wasn't seeing. *What* should *be here and* isn't? he asked himself as he drew.

Once he'd finished, he called to Hadley, 'You can look for your hoodie now, but try to leave everything as you find it.'

'I found this,' Hadley said, holding out a shiny black cylinder. 'It was on the floor, underneath the table in the meeting room.'

'What is it?' Hal took the smooth object and, seeing a crack around the middle, he pulled it apart.

'It's a lipstick.'

Hal twisted the bottom and a tube of fuchsia-pink emerged from the case. 'Good find. Marianne and August Reza don't wear lipstick. This doesn't belong in the Silver Scout.'

'That's what I thought.' Hadley beamed 'Do you think it could be a clue?'

'Hmmmm.' Hal stared at it. 'It could be.' He put it into his pocket. 'I'll see if Mason's found anything.'

'Wow!' Hadley said, stepping into Marianne's room. 'Someone's done a number on this place.'

'I know,' Hal muttered as he walked away. Stepping up into the viewing lounge, he gazed out of the panoramic window into the wide expanse of Middle Park valley, dotted with grazing cattle and blobs of snow. He felt a flash of guilt, thinking of Uncle Nat, on his own, looking at this view from the sightseer lounge.

'Hal,' Mason called. 'Check this out.'

August Reza's bedroom was still clinically tidy. Mason was lying on his back on the floor, his head under the desk.

'What are you doing?' Hal asked.

'Come look.' Mason waved at him. Hal crouched down and peered under the desk. 'This is where the hard drive for the computer should be.' Mason pointed at a large silver box. The back had been prized off, and he was pointing at a rectangular hole. 'I tried to turn the computer on. Nothing happened. I looked, and the hard drive's gone.'

'Maybe August Reza took it with him.'

'Maybe.' Mason wriggled out. 'Although it's kind of a weird thing to do.'

Hadley poked her head up the stairwell. 'The hoodie's not in Marianne's room.' She came up and sat heavily on the sofa with a sigh. 'I guess it's gone forever.' She pulled a sulky face, but then frowned. 'Do you know what's creepy though? Her wardrobe's full of clothes, but her top drawer is empty. It's like someone came and just took her underwear.'

'That's weird.' Hal stepped over Mason's legs, standing on Reza's bed to look out through the domed roof. The Comet's eight carriages were snaking their way along the line in front of him. 'I noticed something else is missing from Marianne's room,' he said. 'Yesterday, Marianne showed me her drawings. The drawing board and the pages she showed me are gone.'

'Maybe her dad took the drawings,' Hadley said. 'You know, for sentimental reasons.'

'But why would he take the drawing board?'

'Who would want to steal Marianne's underwear or her drawings?' Mason asked. 'It's not like they're worth money. Now, the hard drive of August Reza's computer – I'll bet *that's* worth money.'

'If Marianne hadn't been kidnapped,' Hal said, thinking out loud, 'then everyone would still be here in the Silver Scout, right?'

Hadley nodded. 'It's empty because August Reza left the train in Omaha.'

'What if that's *why* she was kidnapped? As a decoy? You said yourself Zircona wouldn't care about ten million dollars – but they *might* care about getting their hands on the designs for August Reza's new solar battery.'

'You think they were on this computer?' Hadley asked.

'I've got it!' Mason rose on to his knees. 'Let's pretend I'm the kidnapper.' He looked at Hal. 'I know you think it was a woman, but say it *was* a man. I grab Marianne, shove her in the trunk of the Chevy, and drive around the corner where I move her to a second car, a getaway car. I change out of the black and into normal clothes, chuck the kidnapper outfit into the getaway car, which then . . . gets away. I walk back to the train and climb aboard. Later that night, I break into this carriage and steal the hard drive. When the train gets to Denver, I meet my Zircona contact and hand over the hard drive in a box, and they pay me with an envelope full of cash.' He looked from Hadley to Hal. 'Cos if that's how it was done, we know *exactly* who that someone is. Don't we?'

CHAPTER TWENTY

THE SEYMOUR SWITCHEROO

The sky was thick with dark clouds that reminded Hal of steam-engine smoke. Granby station was a quaint white wooden building with a green slate roof that sat on a short platform. They jumped down from the Silver Scout, on to the dirt beside the track and ran along to the first sleeping-carriage door and scrambled in.

'If anyone asks, we were in an empty roomette practising magic tricks,' Hadley said, and the others nodded.

'If we're going to catch out Seymour Hart, then we need to do it now, before he goes to lunch,' Mason said.

'Seymour clings to his briefcase and freaks out if anyone touches it,' Hadley said. 'It must have secrets or incriminating evidence inside.'

'What's your idea for how we get to see inside?' Hal asked.

Mason and Hadley grinned at each other, and she said, 'A good old-fashioned switcheroo.'

'First we need to find him,' Mason said. 'I'll go to the other end of the train and work my way back to here.'

'What do you want me to do?' Hal asked.

'Find Francine,' Hadley said. 'Get her to tell you which compartment or roomette Seymour's in.'

Hal nodded. 'What about you?'

'There's something I have to get,' Hadley said mysteriously.

The three of them split up. Hal found Francine in the next sleeping car, stripping the bedding from a vacated roomette.

'Hi, Francine – I wonder if you can help me. Do you know a man called Mr Hart? He's short, thin, grey hair, wears a suit and always carries a briefcase?'

She nodded. 'Mr Seymour Hart.'

'Have you seen him?'

'Not today. He's a quiet kinda man. Bet I don't hear a peep from him till he gets off in Sacramento.'

'He's next to us, isn't he?' asked Hal. 'Roomette nine?'

'No, sugar,' said Francine, chuckling. 'He's not up on this floor. Why'd you want to know where Mr Hart is?'

'He dropped something. I'm trying to return it.'

'Want me to do that for you?' Francine asked. 'It's against the rules for me to give out roomette numbers.'

'No, it's all right. I'll find him at lunch,' Hal said, backing away. 'Thanks, Francine – you're the best.'

'Well, isn't that nice.' Francine beamed at him.

Hal ran to the Morettis' bedroom, where Hadley was waiting for him, holding a briefcase. Her hair was in bunches, and she had on a thick-framed pair of glasses and a jumper he could only guess was her father's. She pulled a geeky face at him.

Hal gawped at the case. 'Is that it?'

'No, doofus. I'm not actually magic. I borrowed this from the luggage rack at the foot of the stairs,' Hadley replied. 'We'll put it back when we're done.'

'No sign of Seymour,' Mason said, as he came down the corridor. 'Did Francine tell you what compartment he's in?'

'She's not allowed, but she did say he was in a roomette on the lower floor and that he's getting off at Sacramento. We can look on the reservation tickets beside the doors for a booking from Chicago to Sacramento. My carriage doesn't have downstairs roomettes, just a bedroom, showers and restrooms. He must be in this carriage.'

The three of them crept down the stairs, past the luggage rack where Hadley had found the dummy case, and peered along the short corridor of roomettes.

Mason tiptoed forward and checked the labels outside each one. 'There's two for Sacramento,' he whispered, 'but that one has ladies' shoes outside.'

'He's travelling alone,' Hal said under his breath. 'I saw him arrive at Chicago station.'

'Then it's the one at the end on the right,' Mason murmured.

'The curtains are shut.' Hadley nodded. 'But look – there's a silhouette. I think it's him.'

'Now what?' Hal looked at them.

'Go and hide in that shower room,' Hadley replied, 'and watch the show.'

Hal did as he was told. Mason nodded, then walked right up to Seymour Hart's roomette door and knocked on the glass, launching into a pitch-perfect imitation of Francine's sing-song voice.

'Good afternoon, Mr Hart!' he called out. 'This is your friendly Amtrak reminder that due to us now being on . . . er . . . West Mountain Time, lunch service will end in ten minutes. You'd better hurry if you don't want to go hungry!' He turned and dashed soundlessly to the shower room, joining Hal, and whispered, 'I heard him curse that he couldn't find his shoes. He's coming out!'

Hal and Mason both looked at Hadley, who'd shoved the borrowed briefcase into the luggage rack and arranged her face into a goofy expression.

The roomette door slid open and Seymour Hart blundered out, pulling on his suit jacket. He grabbed his briefcase and hurried towards Hadley, stuffing a handkerchief into his top pocket.

'There it is!' Hadley said, yanking the borrowed briefcase from the luggage rack, and stumbling backwards as Seymour Hart tried to move past. She cried out as she hit him, tumbling into the stairs, then falling to the floor. The borrowed case clattered to the ground beside her.

Mason winked at Hal.

'Oh m-m-my goodness.' Seymour Hart put his case down to help Hadley up. 'Are you all right? Let me help . . .'

'Argh!' She screamed and flailed her arms, springing to her feet, righting the dummy case. '*Stranger danger! Stranger danger!*' she cried, slapping away his hands. '*Stranger danger!*'

Seymour blinked, staring at her in horror. 'No! I wasn't . . . I just want to help . . . I'm not . . .'

Hal saw Hadley push the dummy case with her foot into the spot where Seymour had set down his own. 'Get off me! Don't touch me!' she shrieked, her bunches flicking wildly. '*GO AWAY!*'

Seymour did not need telling twice: he grabbed the dummy case and dashed up the stairs, heading in the direction of the dining car.

Hadley snatched Seymour's case and ran into the shower room, closing and locking the door. She held up the briefcase, her eyes shining with victory.

'Quick, open it,' Mason said, 'before he notices the switch.'

Hadley put the briefcase flat in the tray of the shower. There were drops of water on the fibreglass floor, and through the plughole Hal could see the ground rushing past.

'It's locked!' Hadley exclaimed, rattling the case in

frustration. 'We didn't think of that . . .'

'He probably has the key in his pocket,' Mason said.

Hadley huffed. '*Now* what are we going to do?'

'I wondered where you'd disappeared to,' Uncle Nat said, looking up at Hal, who stood in the doorway of the roomette with Seymour Hart's briefcase in hands. 'What have you got there?'

'We need your help,' Hal said, indicating Hadley and Mason should come in. It was a squeeze, but Mason slid the door shut behind them as Hadley perched on the arm of Hal's chair. 'This is Seymour Hart's briefcase.' He held it up.

Uncle Nat frowned. 'And Seymour Hart is . . . ?'

'A passenger on the California Comet who we think is involved in Marianne's kidnapping,' Hal replied.

'He's a Zircona spy,' Mason blurted out.

'And how do you come to have his briefcase?' Uncle Nat's eyes narrowed.

'I, err, bumped into him in the corridor,' Hadley said, 'and he accidentally took my case instead of his.'

'*Accidentally?*' Uncle Nat looked at the children, and they all looked down. 'I presume we're discussing how to return it?'

'We were hoping you might help us open it while he's at lunch,' Hal said, wishing he'd confided in his uncle about their investigations earlier. 'We . . . We need to find out if he's involved in the kidnapping.'

'I see.' Uncle Nat took the case from Hal and turned it over, examining the lock. He put it down on the table and drummed his fingers on it, thinking. 'Well, you're right. I do know how to get this case open.'

'You do?' Mason leaned forward eagerly.

'Yes. Everyone out.' Uncle Nat ushered them into the corridor. 'Follow me,' he said, striding off down the carriage, the briefcase swinging by his side.

Hal felt a sickening sense of dread as they headed towards the dining car.

'Is that him?' Uncle Nat pointed at Seymour Hart, sitting at a table by himself, sipping a cup of coffee. Hal nodded.

'Mind if I sit?' Uncle Nat approached the table and slid into the seat opposite Seymour Hart without waiting for a reply.

'What do you want?' Seymour Hart looked anxiously at the three children.

'My nephew told me you bumped into his friend here.' He pointed at Hadley.

'It was an accident.' Seymour looked panicked.

'It seems you made off with her case by mistake.'

'I didn't! I . . .'

Uncle Nat put Seymour's suitcase on to the table. 'And we have yours.'

'What?' Seymour frowned, pulling up the case beside his seat, looking at it properly for the first time. 'I don't believe it! I . . . How did this happen?'

'A mix-up,' said Uncle Nat smoothly, swapping the cases. 'These things happen – all fixed now.'

Seymour Hart clutched his case with both hands.

'Are you all right?' Uncle Nat looked at him with concern.

'My whole life is in this case. If I had lost it . . .' Seymour Hart shuddered.

'If you don't mind me asking –' Uncle Nat gave him a gentle smile – 'what is inside that's so important?'

'Watches,' Seymour Hart replied.

'Watches!' Uncle Nat's eyes lit up.

'I'm on my way to a big conference in Sacramento.' He patted the briefcase. 'I'm a watch salesman. I spent all my savings on the latest models. If I have a good week, that means a good year and a happy family.' He shook his head. 'I really need a good year.'

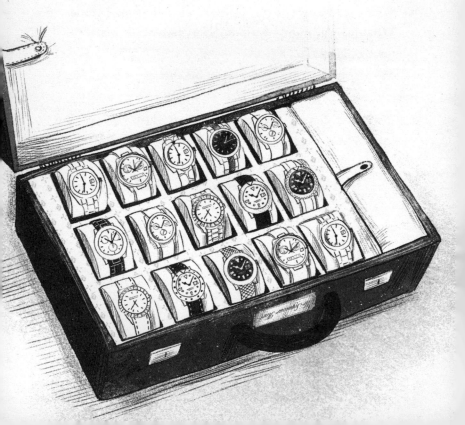

'I'm rather fond of timepieces.' Uncle Nat rolled up his shirt sleeve to show Seymour the three watches on his left wrist. 'Would you be happy to show your watches to an interested customer?'

'Of course!' Seymour Hart slid his coffee out of the way, immediately animated. 'There's always time for watches.' He took a small key from his jacket pocket and popped the lid open.

Mason, Hadley and Hal leaned in, their eyes scouring the case. They saw an impressive display – three rows of expensive-looking wristwatches, each strapped around a velvet cushion sitting in a black box. Shining glass protected elegant clock faces. Cogs and hands precisely measuring the passing of time.

Time that was running out for Marianne.

WINDOW PAINS

Earl slid a plate piled with pasta in front of Hal and delivered giant steaks with fries to Hadley and Mason. 'You kids want any extra sauces?' They all shook their heads.

The Comet was travelling through a deep canyon. Rock as red as brick stretched high above them, blocking any view of the sky. A rushing river ran past on one side of the train; a highway suspended on stilts snaked along the other.

'I can't believe Seymour Hart turned out to be a watch salesman,' Mason said dolefully. 'What a dead end.'

Hal nodded, stabbing his fork into his pasta. He felt like a failure. Marianne hadn't been in the Silver Scout, Ryan hadn't been trying to send him a secret message, and Seymour Hart was a red herring. He kept getting everything wrong. They had no idea who'd kidnapped Marianne or why, and as time ticked away, all he could think about was her losing another tooth. He stared at his fork. He wasn't hungry.

'It was Marianne who pointed the finger at Seymour Hart,'

Hadley said. 'She was the one who said he was a Zircona spy, we weren't to know.'

'Marianne was wrong about Seymour,' Hal said. 'But *someone* was after her.'

'At the time, I thought she might've been making it up to get attention,' Hadley admitted guiltily.

They all stared miserably at their food.

'Do you still think Marianne's on the train?' Mason asked Hal.

'I don't think she can be.' Hal sighed. 'Mason was right: someone would have seen or heard something. And she's not in the Silver Scout.' He shrugged. 'I'm not sure of anything any more.'

They passed a timber yard stacked with logs, yellow planks and piles of wet sawdust. Rain slicked over the window. Hal flicked through the drawings in his sketchbook, hoping something would jump out at him. He got to the page with the *H E L P* scored into the paper, staring at it in disgust before closing the book.

'Ryan was playing with you,' Mason said. 'Must be his idea of a joke.'

'Yeah, well, it's not funny.'

'Not now Marianne's gone,' Hadley agreed.

'I've got a mind to find Ryan and ask him to explain what he thought he was doing,' Hal growled.

'That is a handsome collection of watches Mr Hart has,' Uncle Nat said, sitting down at the table. 'I'm sorely tempted to buy one.' He looked at them. 'Why the sad faces?'

'We were wrong, about everything,' Hal said.

'Nothing wrong with being wrong,' Uncle Nat said. 'However, there *is* something wrong with taking a man's briefcase and trying to open it, even if you did have the best of intentions.'

'There was no other way to find out if he was involved in Marianne's kidnapping,' Mason protested.

'There was.' Uncle Nat picked up the menu.

'How?' Hadley asked.

'By being honest. You should simply have asked Mr Hart some questions about Marianne.'

Hal blinked. 'But we couldn't . . .'

'You could. I asked him politely if he minded showing me what was in his briefcase, and he was happy to oblige.' Uncle Nat stopped Earl as he passed. 'Could I get a green salad . . . and a coffee? Thank you so much.' He looked back at the children. 'I asked cleverly – and, yes, it does help that I'm a grown-up, but I'm certain if you'd asked him the right questions in the right way, he would have opened the case for you too, because he has nothing to hide.'

'I guess.' Mason shrugged.

'Do you know what it is that makes good guys *good*?' Uncle Nat asked, pouring himself a glass of water. 'They defeat the bad guys by sticking to the rules. And that's hard.' He sat back. 'I understand that you want to help Marianne, but don't resort to criminal activity to do it.' He sipped his drink. 'Now, why did you suspect Mr Hart?'

'We saw him give a man a box in Denver station and take an

174

envelope of money,' Hal said. 'We thought it was suspicious, although now we know it was him selling a watch. We were wrong to take his case. I'm sorry, Uncle Nat.'

'Not to worry.' Uncle Nat picked up the borrowed case. 'Although I'll feel a lot better when this is returned to its rightful owner.'

'I took it from the luggage rack,' Hadley said. 'I'll put it back after lunch.'

Mason looked out the window. They had come to a halt among trees dripping with rain. 'Why've we stopped?'

'The line through the Rockies is a single track,' Uncle Nat replied. 'A train must be coming towards us from the other direction. We've pulled over into a passing loop.' He checked a watch on his left wrist. 'I suspect the train coming towards us is the eastbound Comet.'

They heard the chordal blast of a horn, and another silver Comet rattled past the windows. The carriage formation of the other train was different to theirs, with the sleeper carriages beside the luggage car at the front of the train, and the coach cars at the rear. Hal wondered if their formation was different because of August Reza's Silver Scout.

'Isn't it dangerous to have two trains going opposite ways down the same track?' Hal asked.

'Single track is used on routes with a small number of trains travelling along it. As long as the passing loops are long enough for a whole train, it's safe.'

'Shouldn't we be moving on now?' Mason asked.

'Perhaps there's another train,' Uncle Nat said, tucking

into his salad.

Sure enough, a few minutes later, a freight train hauling countless numbers of trucks heaped with aggregate trundled past. Earl appeared and cleared their plates, and they all looked up at the sound of an announcement.

'*Ladies and gentlemen, we've made good time through the mountains and are about to arrive in Glenwood Springs, where we will make a stop of twenty minutes, due to being ahead of schedule. Please enjoy this opportunity to stretch your legs.*'

'Let's go outside,' Mason said eagerly. 'Get off this train for a bit.'

Hal looked at Uncle Nat, who nodded. 'Take your coat. It's raining.'

The brakes sighed as they stopped in Glenwood Springs.

The doors opened, welcoming in the sound of the river that tumbled through the town. Jumping down on to the platform beside Hadley and Mason, Hal felt the patter of light rain on his anorak hood. A concrete bridge reached over the track, and a wide set of steps led to a car park and a bank of payphones.

'There's Gene,' Hal said, pointing.

They watched Gene Jackson climb the steps, heading towards the payphones.

'I wonder who he's calling,' Hadley said. 'Thought everyone had a cell phone these days.'

'I've got an idea!' Hal pulled out his sketchbook. 'Stand still.' He leaned the book against Mason's back and wrote furiously, turned the page, and wrote some more. 'Hadley, find me a stone.'

'What for?'

'To throw at the window. Nothing too big. We don't want to break the glass.'

'Will a quarter do?' Hadley put her hand in her pocket and pulled out a silver coin.

'Perfect. Mason, watch Gene.' Hal pulled Hadley over to stand beneath a compartment window. 'This is the one. Throw it. Not too hard now,' he warned as Hadley tossed the coin. It clattered against the glass, and she caught it as it fell.

Ryan appeared, pulling the curtain aside and staring down at them. He'd obviously been reading, and was clutching a book of *Tintin* stories.

Hal waved and Ryan waved back.

Hal thrust his sketchbook up over his head, open at a page

upon which he'd written:

DO YOU REMEMBER HAVING LUNCH WITH ME YESTERDAY?

Ryan nodded.

Hal flipped the page over, still holding the book aloft. *YOU WROTE IN MY BOOK.*

Ryan frowned.

Hal turned the page. WAS IT A JOKE?

Ryan stared at the question, then looked blankly at Hal and nodded his head.

Hal turned another page. *DID YOU KNOW MARIANNE REZA WAS GOING TO BE KIDNAPPED?*

Ryan shook his head violently.

Hal flipped back the pages till he found the scored secret message he'd discovered in the museum in Omaha. He held it above his head and looked accusingly at Ryan.

Ryan jerked back, shocked by the sight of the page. A figure appeared behind him. He spun around, and they all gasped as Gene glared out the window at them.

'Mason,' Hal hissed. 'You were supposed to be watching him.'

Gene Jackson reached forward and whipped the curtain shut.

CHAPTER TWENTY-TWO

THE HOUDINI
HOODIE

'Do you think we got Ryan in trouble?' Hadley asked nervously, as they walked away.

'I hope not,' Hal replied, though he suspected Gene Jackson was not a kind father.

'Do you think he's being forced to stay in his cabin?' Mason asked. 'Like a prisoner?'

No one replied. Hal was still puzzling over the shocked look on Ryan's face when he'd seen his own secret message. It was like he didn't know it existed. The train's horn blew, calling its passengers aboard.

'C'mon, let's go . . .' Hadley stopped dead.

'What is it?' Mason looked at his sister.

'HEY!' Hadley shouted along the platform. 'HEY! WAIT!' She started running.

'Why are we running?' Hal asked, as he and Mason sprinted after her.

'I don't know,' Mason replied. 'Hadley!' They caught up,

and Mason grabbed his sister. 'What's going on?'

'Didn't you see?'

'See what?'

'That boy was wearing my purple hoodie.'

They stared at each other as the horn sounded again.

'Are you sure?' said Mason.

Hadley nodded. 'He went in coach.'

All the hairs on the back of Hal's neck lifted. 'Then we have to find him,' he said, jumping on to the train.

'How did that kid get his hands on my hoodie?' Hadley wondered, as they rushed through the dining car, dodging around Earl.

'We're about to find out,' Mason said, as they burst through the connecting door, running from one end of the sightseer lounge to the other.

The air in coach smelt of cheese-and-chive crisps. Seats were in pairs either side of the aisle. A baby cried, mewling like a cat, but most passengers wore headphones and didn't seem to notice. Hal whipped out his sketchbook and drew outlines of the passengers in their seats.

Mason put his finger to his lips and pointed. Adalbert Cabbage was sat on the right of the aisle, her chair tipped back, snoring. She was wrapped in her enormous blue puffer coat and wore an eye mask. Julio the lizard was lying across her collarbone, staring up at them. The seat beside her was unoccupied, a small backpack covered in comic-book characters dumped on to it. As he sketched Adalbert, Hal wondered if she really was dangerous.

A sweep of the top floor of the carriage yielded no purple hoodie, so they went downstairs. Mason grabbed Hadley and pointed. Sitting in an aisle seat halfway down the carriage, his fingers hammering away at the buttons on a games console, was a young boy wearing Hadley's precious jumper.

Hadley pushed past Hal, striding down the aisle. 'Hey.' She greeted the boy with a perfunctory smile. 'That's my top, and I'd like it back.'

The boy sank lower in his chair. He wasn't much older than nine or ten. The jumper was big on him. He glared at Hadley with distrusting brown eyes, and pulled the hood up over his tight black curls before returning to his game.

Hadley leaned down, insistent. 'Hey, you're wearing *my* sweater.'

'No, I'm not,' the boy said, his eyes glued to his game.

'Yes, you—'

'Finders, keepers. Losers, weepers.'

'Hello.' Hal pulled Hadley back. 'My name's Harrison. What's yours?'

'Derek,' the boy muttered.

'Hi, Derek.' Hal smiled as the boy looked up from his game. 'Is that your mum?' He nodded at the woman asleep next to Derek, head resting against the window. She had a pair of noise-cancelling headphones clamped over her thicket of hair.

Derek nodded. 'Mom's tired. We boarded late last night.'

'Do you think she'd mind if I bought you a drink and something to eat in the cafe?' Hal asked.

Derek looked up at Hal, suddenly interested. 'Can I have a candy bar?'

'You can have whatever you want,' Hadley said.

Hal led Derek into the sightseer lounge and down to the cafe, Mason and Hadley following behind.

'You talk strange,' Derek said to Hal.

'I'm from England,' Hal replied, smiling. 'What would you like from the counter?'

After buying Derek his choice of snacks, they sat down at the booth that they now thought of as their table.

'Purple.' Mason nodded at Derek, as he devoured his Hershey bar. 'Interesting choice of colour for a sweater.'

Derek scowled. 'I like purple.'

'Do you know who Houdini was?' Hadley asked.

'Sure. He was the greatest espa-cologist who ever lived,' Derek replied, giving her a chocolatey smile.

'Escapologist,' Mason corrected.

'That's what I said.'

'Can I tell you a story?' Hadley asked.

Derek shrugged and slurped his carton of juice.

'I met a girl, on this train, at this table. She said she was being followed by a man and that she needed a disguise to escape him. I was wearing my favourite hoodie. My pop gave it to me for my birthday. He had bought a purple sweater – it's my favourite colour – and printed a quote from Houdini on the front, because Houdini's my hero.' She looked pointedly at him. 'There's no other top like it in the world.'

'Why's Houdini your hero?'

'I'm a magician, and he was the best.'

'You're a magician?'

Hadley made a show of checking to see if anyone was watching. Then she reached behind Derek's ear and pulled out a coin. Derek gave her a withering look, obviously unimpressed. She transferred the coin to her other hand and slammed her hand flat against the table. They heard a jangling sound. She showed him her empty hand and then pulled her other hand from under the table. It was full of quarters.

Derek's mouth fell open.

Hadley rattled the quarters under his nose. 'Want another Hershey bar?' Derek nodded. 'OK, but first I want to hear the story of how you got *your* hoodie –' she smiled – 'because the girl who took *my* hoodie promised she would give it back. But she can't, because she was kidnapped.'

Derek blinked. 'That Reza girl?' He tugged at the top. 'She had this?'

Hadley, Mason and Hal all nodded. Derek swallowed.

'I found it, stuffed in the trash can in the restroom.'

'When did you find it?' All Hal's senses were alert.

'We boarded the train in McCook. I needed to, you know,

go, so I went to the restroom. I saw this sweater in the trash. It was the only thing in there, apart from a few paper towels. It seemed clean, and I was cold, so I put it on.' He looked down at it. 'Here –' he wriggled his arms out of the sleeves and pulled it over his head – 'you can have it back.'

'Oh thank you,' said Hadley, hugging it.

'You got on in McCook?' Hal closed his eyes, bringing up an image of the train timetable. 'So, you found this at four o'clock in the morning?'

'Uh-huh. It was real early.'

'Did you see anyone get off at McCook? Like a grown-up and a girl? Or several grown-ups with a girl?'

Derek shook his head. 'I didn't see anyone. Look, I have to get back to Mom before she wakes up and freaks that I'm not there.' He stood up. 'Thanks for the candy. It's been . . . weird.'

'Bye, Derek,' Hadley called after him. 'Thanks.'

'Now we have another mystery to solve,' Hal said, looking at Hadley. 'How did your hoodie end up in the bin, in the coach restroom, in the middle of the night?'

'I don't care.' Hadley buried her face in the hoodie. 'Eurrghhh, it smells of boy.'

'You gave Marianne that hoodie. She wore it to the Silver Scout, where she got changed into a yellow dress, which she was wearing when she was kidnapped.' Hal shook his head. 'So how did the hoodie get from the Silver Scout to the coach restroom?'

'Maybe it *escaped*. Like Houdini?' Mason joked.

185

'Don't you see? It's impossible.' Hal opened his sketchbook and took out the sweet wrapper. 'Just like these sweets.' He felt a thrill of excitement. 'Something really *is* going on on this train and we're going to find out what it is.'

CHAPTER TWENTY-THREE

A CRISIS OF CONFIDENCE

'We need to tell a grown-up,' Hadley said, as they walked back through the train.

'Who's going to believe us?' Hal replied.

'What about your uncle?' Mason suggested.

'You saw how angry he got about Seymour Hart's briefcase. If he knew I'd gone into the Silver Scout, he'd never take me on a train trip again. We can't tell him.'

'He didn't get *that* mad.'

'But I didn't tell him when Marianne pulled my hair, or about her giving Woody the slip. I haven't even told him about Ryan's stupid drawing.' He threw his hands up. 'I can't blurt it all out. It sounds childish. And he'll think . . . He'll think I've been hiding things from him.' Hal didn't know why he hadn't told his uncle these things and he wished he had. But there'd never been a good time.

'OK, not your uncle,' Hadley said.

'Dad'll crack a joke and tell us to talk to the police,' said Mason.

187

'Why don't we?' Hadley asked.

'The police won't listen.' Hal scowled. 'They'll pat us on the head and tell us to run along and play like good little children.' He shoved his hands into his trouser pockets. His fist bumped against the lipstick that Hadley had found in the Silver Scout. An idea popped into his head. 'Let's tell Zola. She knows I've solved a case before. She'll listen.'

'But she's one of our suspects,' Mason pointed out. 'Can we trust her?'

Hal thought about this. 'If Uncle Nat trusts her, then so do I, but we'll watch her closely. If she is involved, she might give herself away.'

'You're the detective,' Hadley said.

'Cool. Let's go.'

Hal led his friends to Zola's compartment and knocked on her door.

Zola looked surprised to see the three of them standing there.

'Hello.' Hal smiled. 'These are my friends, Mason and Hadley. Please may we come in? We need to talk to you.'

'Is everything OK?' Zola ushered them in.

Hal looked at Mason and Hadley as they sat down on Zola's sofa. 'We've been investigating the kidnapping.'

'Have you now?' Zola sounded immediately interested. 'Found anything?'

'We're not sure.' Hal pulled the lipstick out of his pocket. 'Is this yours?'

Zola took it, pulled the cap off, and twisted the stick up.

188

'It's pink,' she said. 'I only wear red.' She puckered her red lips together, making a kissing noise.

Good, Hal thought, feeling a wave of relief. There was no evidence to place Zola in the Silver Scout after the kidnapping. 'I wanted to ask you about what Marianne said to you before she was kidnapped . . .'

'Are you interrogating *me*?' Zola's voice became flinty.

'No, I—'

'Did Nathaniel put you up to this? Doesn't he believe me?'

'He definitely does believe you,' Hal replied hastily, 'and he doesn't know we're here.'

'I'm glad someone believes me,' Zola said, sitting down in the armchair. 'Rodriguez is following me around like a bad smell.'

'Vanessa Rodriguez?'

'She's a cop,' Zola said. 'Thought you would've worked that out.'

'I see.' Hal nodded. The conversation he'd had earlier with Vanessa about Adalbert Cabbage suddenly made sense.

'So, why are you here?' Zola asked.

Hal looked her in the eyes. 'We think Marianne, or at least one of the kidnappers, is on this train.'

'What?' Zola rose a little in her chair and then sat back down. 'Do you have proof? What makes you think that?' Hal could see her mind whirring. 'What does Nathaniel say?'

Hal looked at the floor. 'I haven't told him.'

'Why?'

'I worked out the door code to the Silver Scout . . .'

'Clever boy!' Zola sounded impressed.

'And we snuck in, to search for clues . . .' Hal paused, waiting to be told off.

'Yes? And?'

'Well, we've done something illegal, haven't we?' Hal looked up. 'Uncle Nat will be cross.'

Zola's face cracked into a wide smile and she laughed raucously. 'Oh Harrison, your uncle's not a saint – he's a journalist! Sure, he's a travel journalist who writes about trains most of the time, but if you think he's never snuck in somewhere he shouldn't have, you're mistaken.' She leaned forward. 'Now, tell me what you've found.'

'Marianne's bedroom has been turned over,' Hal replied.

'Burgled, or just messy?'

Hal looked at Hadley.

'Burgled,' she said. 'But *weird* burgled. I checked the drawers. There are lots of clothes, but no underwear. Those drawers are empty.'

'Her drawing board and pages are gone too,' Hal said.

Zola frowned. 'Strange things to steal.'

'And the hard drive from August Reza's computer has been taken,' Mason added.

'*What?!*' Zola's eyes grew wide. 'But that'll have the designs for his new solar battery!'

'We think the kidnap could've been a diversion to empty the Silver Scout so someone could get to Reza's computer,' Hal said. 'Mason pointed out the ransom is small for a man as rich as August Reza.'

190

Mason beamed proudly.

'How d'you know what the ransom is?' Zola said. 'It's not been published.'

'I copied down the ransom note,' Hal admitted.

'Cos he's freakin' Sherlock da Vinci,' crowed Mason.

Zola raised her eyebrows. 'And who do you think wants that hard drive?'

'Zircona,' said Hal.

'It won't be Zircona,' said Zola, frowning. 'But you said you think Marianne is on the train?'

'We found something only Marianne could have dropped, and the only time she could've dropped it was after the kidnapping. I thought she was being held in the Silver Scout – that's why we went there – but she wasn't . . .'

The train slowed, passing bright-yellow service carriages parked in sidings as they approached Grand Junction station.

'And there's something else,' Hal continued. 'Yesterday afternoon, Marianne borrowed Hadley's purple hoodie –' Hadley held it up – 'and wore it to the Silver Scout. Then Marianne changed into, and was seen being kidnapped in, a yellow dress a few hours later. But this hoodie was found in a restroom in coach at four o'clock this morning.'

Zola examined the hoodie. 'What's your theory, Hal?'

'We don't have one that fits,' Hal admitted. 'That's why we came to you. Uncle Nat says you're really good at your job . . .'

'Does he?' Zola smiled. 'That's nice to hear.'

'We thought you might help us. We can't go to the police without evidence. They won't take us seriously.'

'I'm in.' Zola nodded at Hal. 'Breaking this story could win me a Pulitzer Prize.'

'We're at Grand Junction,' Mason said, looking out of the window as the train stopped. 'Hey, check out the mobsters in sunglasses.'

'Start at the beginning,' said Zola, setting her phone down between them and turning on the audio recorder. 'Tell me everything, right from when you boarded the train in Chicago.'

But before Hal could begin, there was a curt knock on the door and a deep, clear voice rang out. 'FBI, open up!'

Mason and Hadley gasped, jumping to their feet as the door opened. A towering man in a charcoal suit stood beside a middle-aged woman with short curly hair. A gold badge dangled on a chain over her lilac blouse, and the man had the same badge clipped to his belt. They both wore dark glasses, and Hal realized he was holding his breath. But to his surprise, Zola laughed.

'I should have known they'd bring you two in,' she said.

The FBI officers removed their glasses, their faces creased with smiles of familiarity.

'Guys, this is Agent Lena Kowalski and Agent Malcolm Balewa from the FBI,' Zola said, beckoning them inside. 'I'm afraid there's not much room.'

'The real FBI?' Hal's voice had tightened to a squeak.

'I didn't know you'd become a schoolteacher, Zola.' Agent Kowalski eyed Hal curiously.

'These are my friends,' Zola explained. 'Hal, Hadley and Mason.'

'Did you make friends with Marianne Reza, too?' Agent Balewa's voice was so low it sounded like an earthquake.

'I've known her father for years,' said Zola. 'They put you on the kidnapping case?'

Agent Balewa nodded.

'Have you found Marianne?' Hal asked eagerly. 'Do you know where she is?'

'Not yet, kid,' Agent Kowalski replied. 'Zola, we have to ask you some questions. We're holding the train.' She looked at Hal, Mason and Hadley. 'Your friends should leave.'

Without a moment's hesitation, Hadley and Mason scurried out of the compartment. But Hal didn't follow. 'Zola had nothing to do with the kidnapping,' he said, boldly stepping forward.

'It's alright Hal,' Zola put her hand on his arm. 'I've worked with Kowalski and Balewa before.'

'You interviewed us,' Balewa corrected her, 'we never worked together.'

'Really?' Zola fixed him with a hard stare. 'Remind me to tell your superiors how you really solved the Trasker case.'

Balewa cleared his throat and looked at the floor. Kowalski grinned, and Hal realized the agents knew Zola well.

'I told the police in Omaha everything I saw,' Zola said, standing up. 'I've nothing more to say.'

'The investigation crosses state lines,' Balewa said. 'It's an FBI matter now.'

'And I'm your number one suspect?' Zola cocked her head.

'You're our number one witness,' Balewa countered.

'You know how this goes. We need to bring you in for a full interview.'

Zola sighed. 'Can I leave my things on the train?'

'Sure.' Kowalski nodded. 'We'll have everything collected in Emeryville.'

'If anything gets damaged, I'll expect compensation.' Zola pointed at them, and Balewa gave a great booming laugh.

'You haven't changed one bit.'

'Go on, admit it.' Zola winked at him. 'You missed me.'

'Let's go,' Kowalski said, stepping out into the corridor.

Zola turned to Hal, taking his hands. 'Go to your uncle. Tell him everything. He won't be angry.' She gave him an encouraging smile and then followed Balewa out the door.

Hal looked down. Zola had pushed her watch into his palm. He stared at it for a second, then shoved it into his pocket, hurrying after them.

'I should warn you,' Zola was saying to Balewa as they descended the stairs, 'I won't say a word without my lawyer.'

'Call him when we get to the airfield,' Balewa replied, putting his sunglasses back on.

'Call *her*,' Zola corrected him. 'I'll call *her* when we get to the airfield, thank you.'

'Ooff,' Kowalski chuckled as they stepped off the train. 'You walked right into that one.'

CHAPTER TWENTY-FOUR

YORKSHIRE GOLD

'Uncle Nat! Zola's been arrested!' Hal cried, bolting through the door of their roomette.

'*What?*' Uncle Nat jumped to his feet. 'Where is she?'

They wobbled, grabbing on to their chairs as the train lurched out of Grand Junction.

Hal pointed out the window as the platform slid away.

'Two FBI agents came, and they said they had to take her off the train to ask her some questions. I told them she didn't have anything to do with the kidnapping.'

'You were with her? Is she all right?'

'She seemed okay,' Hal admitted. 'She said she was their number one suspect, and they said she was the number one witness.'

'Did they read her her rights?' Uncle Nat asked.

Hal shook his head.

'Then she hasn't been arrested.'

'She seemed to know them. She kept teasing Agent Balewa.'

'Malcolm Balewa?' Uncle Nat looked relieved. 'He and Zola

are old friends.' He sat down. 'But why were you with her?'

Hal took a deep breath, his fingers nervously intertwining. 'I was investigating Marianne's kidnapping.'

'Ah yes.' Uncle Nat took off his glasses, polishing them with the corner of his jumper as he smiled at Hal. 'You and the Morettis have been haring up and down the train like dogs chasing sticks. You seem to have got over your homesickness.'

'You knew I was homesick?' Hal said in a small voice.

'Well, no. I assumed you were. It's only natural. First time so far away from home.' He put his glasses back on. 'America can be overwhelming.'

'But *you're* at home here.'

'I am now –' Uncle Nat leaned forward – 'but you should have seen me the first time I came to America.' He shook his head. 'I hated it. I missed home so much that I cried.'

'You *cried?*' Hal was amazed. 'I don't hate America – I think it's brilliant – but it's so different from home. I miss my stuff, my room, my family, and Bailey.'

'Which is wonderful.'

'It's wonderful to be homesick?'

'Yes, because when you get off the plane and see your parents, you'll run to them and hug them to bits. You don't feel like that when you get home from school, do you?' Hal shook his head. Uncle Nat smiled. 'You only feel that way about your family and your home when you've travelled far from them.'

Hal considered this and felt a bit better about being homesick. 'I guess.'

'Homesickness isn't bad,' Uncle Nat said. 'It's a thing you

have to get used to if you're going to travel.'

Hal smiled, thinking how glad he was to be travelling with his uncle.

'Now, you sit there.' Uncle Nat stood up and rummaged in his holdall. 'I've got just the thing to help us think.' He pulled out a freezer bag.

'Tea bags?'

'Not just any tea bags – these are Yorkshire Gold.' Uncle Nat shook the bag. 'I never leave England without them. I'll make us a nice cup of tea, and you can tell me about your investigations.'

After Uncle Nat had left, Hal noticed a small key on the floor. One of the suitcase padlock keys had fallen from his uncle's jacket. He picked it up and put it in his pocket to keep it safe. He got his sketchbook, and laid it on the table, ready to tell his Uncle Nat everything. Looking out the window at the churning Colorado River, he waited for his uncle to return. A cliff of orange oxidized earth rose from the far bank, and he thought he could be on an alien planet.

Uncle Nat returned, placing two steaming cups of tea on the table. Hal blew on his before he took a sip. The hot drink was comforting. 'It tastes different to tea back home.'

'One of the mysteries of travel is that milk tastes different everywhere,' said Uncle Nat. 'French milk is different from Italian milk, and so on. Nothing ever matches the taste of a cup of tea made at home, but this is close enough to make me happy.'

They drank their tea in silence, and Hal became aware that

Uncle Nat was waiting for him to talk.

'I don't know where to start. There's lots I haven't told you. I was so angry with you for not watching Marianne,' Hal admitted. 'I wanted to solve this without you.'

'I understand,' Uncle Nat said quietly. 'Why don't you start at the beginning, at Union Station in Chicago?'

Hal opened his sketchbook, telling his uncle about his first meeting with Marianne. He described how angry she'd become later, when he knocked over her pens, and how she'd disguised herself when she came to apologize. He talked

about Ryan's strange behaviour at lunch; how Marianne had pointed the finger at Seymour Hart, saying he was a Zircona spy; and how Hadley had lent Marianne the Houdini hoodie. The story poured out of Hal as he flicked through the pages of the sketchbook. He hesitated, then confessed he'd worked out the door code to the Silver Scout, and showed his uncle the drawing of Marianne's messy bedroom. Then he explained how Hadley's hoodie had turned up in coach, on Derek.

'I think Marianne is on this train,' Hal said. 'I know it doesn't make sense, but neither does the sweet wrapper or that hoodie.'

Uncle Nat looked stunned. 'I don't know what to say!' He shook his head. 'You say Reza's hard drive is missing? Who do you think took it?'

'We thought it must be a spy from the Zircona corporation, but Zola said . . .' Hal suddenly remembered her watch and pulled it from his pocket. 'Zola's watch – she gave it to me before she left the train.'

'I wonder why?' Uncle Nat took it from Hal and examined it. 'It's a Zircona smartwatch.'

'She gave it to me and told me to come and tell you everything.'

Uncle Nat looked over his glasses at Hal. 'You went to Zola before coming to me?'

Hal felt his cheeks burning. 'I . . . I . . . I'm sorry. You were so cross about Seymour's briefcase switch that I was scared to tell you I'd been into the Silver Scout in case you didn't want to take me travelling again.'

'I don't think I got cross.' Uncle Nat sat back. 'I wanted

you to understand that there are other ways of doing things – ways that won't get you into trouble. I'm responsible for you, Hal, and if anything happens to you, while you're in my care, I'll have to answer to Bev. Your mum can be pretty frightening.'

'I know.' Hal grinned.

'Well, let's work out why Zola gave you her watch.' Uncle Nat pressed a button on its side and then tapped the illuminated screen. 'Here are her messages.' He swiped through them shaking his head. 'Hmmm, perhaps her emails . . .'

Minutes of silence ticked past as Uncle Nat scanned the screen, and then he looked at Hal. 'Bingo! Do you want to know how Zola knew the kidnappers weren't working for Zircona?'

Hal nodded.

'Because *she* is. I rather suspect that's why she's been taken in for questioning. This email chain explains what she'll be paid for gathering information. It seems they're concerned Reza might use his solar batteries in self-driving cars.'

'Zola's working for Zircona!' Hal was shocked. '*She's* the spy?'

'Someone must've tipped off the FBI that Zola was on the Zircona payroll.'

'They think Zola was the person who led Marianne outside into the waiting arms of the kidnappers.'

'Except she didn't,' Uncle Nat said firmly. 'It was Marianne who asked Zola to go outside.' He lifted the watch. 'Her

Zircona contact sent her a message this morning expressing horror at the crime, instructing Zola to help in any way she can. Zircona aren't involved.'

'Then who stole the hard drive?' Hal frowned. 'And what's the real motive for the kidnapping?'

'The ransom note on its own suggests a financial motive,' Uncle Nat said.

'But why is the amount so small? Surely August Reza would pay billions?'

'I don't know.' Uncle Nat sighed.

'We're running out of time.' Hal stood up. 'If Marianne is somewhere on this train, then we've got to find her before she loses another tooth, and Zola gets the blame. Bits of the puzzle are missing, but we've got a better chance of figuring it out if we're all working together.'

'Together?'

'Yes – come on.' Hal grabbed his sketchbook and charged out of the roomette.

CHAPTER TWENTY-FIVE

SUSPICIOUS MINDS

Rapping on the door of the Morettis' bedroom, Hal and his uncle were greeted by Mason.

'We were about to come invite you to a party,' said Mason.

'A party?'

'To celebrate our last night on the train.' Hadley's face popped up. 'What do you think about Zola being taken away by the FBI?' She waved them in.

'Zola's working for Zircona', Hal said, 'but that doesn't mean she's got anything to do with the kidnapping.'

'Zola is the Zircona spy!' Mason exclaimed.

'But she's *not* a kidnapper?' Hadley asked.

'So it would seem,' Uncle Nat replied.

Hadley and Mason looked at Hal.

'I told him everything. He's going to help us.' Hal looked around. 'Why is it so tidy in here?'

'We packed,' Mason said. 'We get off in Reno at eight tomorrow morning.'

Hal's heart sank. He didn't want to say goodbye to the Morettis.

Flattening the seats into a double mattress, Hadley sat cross-legged on it, and Mason and Hal joined her as Uncle Nat closed the door and sat in the armchair.

Hal put his sketchbook down beside him on the bed. 'Four heads are better than two. I thought if we went over the clues together, we might be able to work out where Marianne is before she loses another tooth.'

'Let's do it,' Hadley said.

'Always a pleasure to work with the great Sherlock da Vinci.' Mason winked.

'Don't call me that.' Hal gave him a friendly shove. 'So far, I've solved nothing.'

The door opened and Frank Moretti threw his hands in the air. 'Hey! You came to our party.'

'I thought you were getting food?' Hadley looked accusingly at her father's empty hands.

'Food's coming,' Frank reassured her. 'What are we doing? Board games?'

'We're going to solve the kidnapping of Marianne Reza,' Mason replied.

'Well now, peanut –' Frank sat down on the bed beside his son – 'that's some serious business.'

'Yes, it is.' Hal opened his sketchbook. 'If we can figure out how Hadley's hoodie ended up in the bin, in coach, at four in the morning –' he looked up – 'that will be the key to working out who's got Marianne.'

'I have a theory.' Hadley sat up, enjoying the sudden attention. 'At the press conference, Marianne was wearing a yellow dress, and at seven thirty she was driven away wearing that dress . . .'

'Wait . . .' Frank held up his hand. 'Your hoodie, Hadley? I saw it.' Everyone looked at him. 'In the commotion at Omaha, I was rushing through the train looking for you. I was in a panic. I saw a kid in coach wearing a purple hoodie, with the hood up. I called out your name – the kid glanced back. It wasn't you, so I kept looking, but I was surprised because it looked like your hoodie.'

'Are you sure it was the same hoodie?' Uncle Nat asked.

Frank shrugged. 'Can't be certain. I never saw the front, just the back. I was kinda frantic. But it looked the same.'

'Was it a boy or girl wearing it?' Mason asked.

'Not sure,' said Frank apologetically. 'The kid was wearing glasses.'

'It wasn't Derek,' Hadley said. 'He didn't get on the train till four in the morning.'

'Derek's the kid who found it in the trash?' Frank asked, and they all nodded.

There was a long silence as they puzzled over this new information.

'Do you have any other clues?' Uncle Nat asked. 'Sometimes one clue in combination with another makes sense of both.'

'The sweet wrapper.' Hal pulled it from his sketchbook. 'Only Marianne has these French sweets, but it had to have been dropped between six o'clock in the evening and six in the morning, otherwise Francine would have swept it up.'

'There's the missing hard drive,' Mason said, 'which has either been stolen, or –' he shrugged – 'August Reza took it with him.'

'And the pink lipstick,' Hadley said.

Hal pulled it out of his pocket, taking off the lid.

'You know who has lips that colour, which I wouldn't mind smooching?' Frank waggled his eyebrows, and his ears twitched. 'Adie Cabbage. She's hot stuff.'

'Pop!' Mason and Hadley exclaimed in horror.

Hal looked at Uncle Nat, remembering the conversation they'd both had with Vanessa Rodrigucz.

The Comet slowed down, and Frank jumped to his feet. 'I'll be right back,' he said, dashing from the room as the train wheezed to a halt.

'Where are we?' asked Hal, looking out the window.

'Helper,' said Uncle Nat.

Behind the rocky horizon, the sun was sending out flares of gold into the darkening sky.

'It's a railway town,' his uncle continued. 'Trains used stop here to add an extra locomotive, help them make it up the hill. They were called *helper* trains, hence the name of the town.'

'I see where you get your nerdery from,' Mason whispered to Hal.

'Look!' Hadley pointed out the window. 'What is Pop doing?'

They crowded round, watching as Frank dashed into the car park and handed a wad of dollar bills to a young man

on a moped in return for a stack of enormous pizza boxes. 'He got pizza!' Hadley clapped. 'Aww, Pop's the greatest.' Frank Moretti sprinted back to the train as the horn went. They greeted him with cheers when he entered the bedroom triumphantly carrying his tower of boxes. 'Delivery guy hadn't ever delivered to a train station before,' he said, handing out the pizzas. 'He thought I was loco. Ha! *Loco!* Get it?' He chuckled.

They tucked into pizzas the size of car wheels, dripping with cheese and spicy pepperoni.

'If there's pizza in heaven,' Hal said, '*this* is what it'll taste like.'

After dinner, as the Comet picked up speed again, Hadley set up three paper cups, making a ball from scrunched-up tin foil. Hal laughed at the puzzled expression on his uncle's face as she used the French Drop to make one ball become two, and then two become one big ball, which she then made disappear.

'I once saw a disappearing trick at the Adelphi Theatre that I have never forgotten,' Uncle Nat told her. 'Someone from the audience was invited on stage to inspect a wardrobe – which they did – and then the magician's assistant got inside. A sheet was thrown over the wardrobe, and when they pulled it away, the audience member was inside the wardrobe, and the assistant was sat in the audience!'

'I know how that's done!' Hadley beamed.

'If Marianne's kidnapping were a magic trick,' Hal said, 'how would you do it?'

'Kidnapping isn't an act of magic, Hal. It has a victim,' Hadley said. 'Magic is a harmless lie, one that everyone involved agrees to, including the audience. When you go to a magic show, you *want* to be tricked.'

'Talking of shows –' Frank stood up and cracked his knuckles. 'Seeing as tonight's a special occasion, how about a song?' He grabbed a suit bag from the hook on the back of the door and stepped into the shower room.

Hadley and Mason exchanged an alarmed look, then turned to Hal and Uncle Nat with forced smiles.

'Everything OK?' Hal asked.

'Pop doesn't look *exactly* like him,' Mason said in a low voice.

'Or sound like him,' Hadley added in a whisper.

'But he's really good,' they both said together.

There was a bang and they all jumped as Frank leaped out of the shower room dressed in a white leather onesie studded with sparkling rhinestones, a black wig with a huge quiff, and a pair of oversized sunglasses. Pointing a finger to the ceiling, he curled his lip saying, '*Uh-huh*,' before launching into a song about a hound dog crying, and frantically wiggling his hips. At the end, he dropped on to one knee and threw his arms wide.

Hadley and Mason whooped and applauded, and after a stunned moment, Hal and Uncle Nat did the same.

Frank pulled off his sunglasses, his expression eager. 'Did you think the King was in the room?'

'The King?' Hal asked.

'The King! Elvis! The greatest singer that ever lived.'

'Oh, yeah,' Hal said, uncertain.

'That was an unforgettable performance,' Uncle Nat said warmly. 'Bravo.'

*

It was getting late when Hal and his uncle finally said goodnight to the Morettis, agreeing to meet for a goodbye breakfast in the morning. As the train thundered through Utah, Hal brushed his teeth in the downstairs restroom and put on his pyjamas. It had been an eventful day, but he was no closer to working out what had happened to Marianne, and he was worried about Zola. As he clambered into his bunk and slipped under the crackly blue blanket, the Comet's horn rose mournfully above the rumble of the air conditioning. The bunk rocked gently as the train picked up speed through the flat country. When he closed his eyes, the vision of a scared Marianne was waiting for him once more in the darkness.

'I'm going to find you,' he promised her.

CHAPTER TWENTY-SIX

ALL THE WAY
TO RENO

When Hal woke, he found Uncle Nat sitting up in the lower bunk, gazing out of the window at the sunrise.

'Morning Hal,' he said, taking a sip of his coffee. 'Come and look at this view. The Nevada desert. Nothing and no one for hundreds of miles.'

Hal slithered down from his bunk with his blanket and sat at the foot of his uncle's bed. 'Hadley and Mason leave this

morning.' He sighed, staring out at the sandy scrubland.

'We'll be getting off the train ourselves this afternoon,' Uncle Nat pointed out. 'Which reminds me, I need to put my watch back another hour. We're on pacific time now.'

'All these time zones make me dizzy.' Hal rubbed his eyes. 'What time is it now?'

'It's six,' Uncle Nat said, twiddling the knob on his American watch.

Hal stared out at the candyfloss clouds hovering over the desert plains. 'I'm going to check on Ryan today. Make sure he's OK.'

'Good idea.' Uncle Nat nodded.

'I'd planned to fill my sketchbook with pictures of the train and the landscape, but I've been so desperate to find Marianne, it's ended up being a lot of passenger sketches.'

'Perhaps, once the Morettis have left, you should take time to sketch something else. It might help you think.'

Hal nodded. 'I can't make the pieces of the puzzle fit.'

'You can't solve every mystery, Hal.' Uncle Nat shrugged.

'I want to know that Marianne's all right,' Hal said, as telephone wires rose and dipped alongside the track. Clumps of sickly-looking grass sprouted through the desert's sand-baked crust. It was the first desert Hal had ever seen, and all he could think about was a girl who'd pulled his hair.

When Hal and his uncle arrived at the dining car later that morning, the Morettis were already seated. Frank was sitting across the aisle from Hadley and Mason, and he waved at Uncle Nat. 'Thought we'd leave the kids to their fun, Nathaniel. You want coffee?'

'I wish we were going all the way to Emeryville with you,' Hadley said, as Hal sat down.

'Me too.' Mason nodded. 'It's been, you know . . .' For the first time, he seemed to have run out of words.

'I know.' Hal opened his sketchbook to a clean page, and did a quick drawing of Hadley and Mason sitting across the table with a stack of pancakes and bacon in front them. Below it he wrote his address and telephone number. He ripped out the page and pushed it across the table. 'You probably won't visit Crewe, but if you ever come to England, I could get the train to London and meet you.'

Mason pulled Hal's sketchbook over and took his pencil.

'This is the hotel we're staying at in Reno. You call if anything happens.'

'Like what?'

'Like, if you solve the kidnapping, I wanna know!'

Hal smiled, but his mouth dropped as Earl stiffly welcomed Adalbert Cabbage and Julio to the dining car. 'Look who just came in,' he said under his breath.

Earl sat Adalbert beside the door, telling her she'd have to leave with Julio when the carriage filled up. She looked bleary-eyed, and Hal noticed her lips were stained pink. Taking his pencil back from Mason, he drew her in his book as swiftly and accurately as he could.

'Don't both look at once,' Hal whispered, 'but Adalbert's hairline is pale – a white blonde. The red frizzy beehive is a *wig*.'

Mason shoved a pancake into his mouth and dropped his fork to the floor, casually looking at Adalbert as he picked it up. 'You're right!'

'And that coat,' Hal muttered. 'It's huge and long. It must be pretty hot, but she never takes it off.'

'Eat up, kids,' Frank said from across the aisle. 'We've got to finish packing.'

'The Comet waits fifteen minutes at Reno,' Hadley said, as she and Mason got up from their seats. 'Let's go into the station and get a paper. There might be more news about Marianne.'

Hal nodded. 'I'll meet you on the platform.'

Once the Morettis were gone, Uncle Nat came and sat

opposite Hal. 'Do you fancy pancakes?'

'I'm not hungry,' Hal said, staring past his uncle at Adalbert Cabbage. 'My stomach thinks it's night time.'

'What are you drawing?' Uncle Nat looked, then glanced at Adie. 'Ah, I see.'

'I think she's got something to do with the kidnapping,' Hal said under his breath, 'but I don't know what. That was her lipstick Hadley found in the Silver Scout – I'm sure of it . . .'

Reno station was sunk into the ground. The tracks into the city were laid in a deep trough. High concrete walls boxed in the platforms, creating shade in which the waiting passengers stood. Stepping out on to the platform, Hal felt the desert heat cling to his skin. Blinking at the blazing sun, he spotted the Morettis heaving their bags down from the luggage car.

'I'm going to get a newspaper and say goodbye,' he called back to Uncle Nat, who was standing in the doorway of the train. Hal ran to join Hadley and Mason. The three of them weaved through the crowd to the main building.

'Look. There's a kiosk over there.' Hadley pulled a handful of change from her pocket and went over to buy a *Los Angeles Times*. She held up the paper as Hal and Mason joined her. Marianne was still front-page news.

'They've pulled out another tooth!' Hal gasped, reading the headline. The article described how a second tooth had been delivered to Reza Technologies in the early hours of the morning.

Mason took the paper from Hadley and scanned the page, shaking his head in shock. 'Those kidnappers really mean business.'

'I don't understand,' Hal muttered. 'This doesn't make sense.'

'I don't think she can be on the train.' Hadley said gently.

'Hal!' Uncle Nat called down the platform and Hal waved back.

'I've got to go.' Hal looked at Mason and Hadley, suddenly feeling awkward.

'I guess this is it,' said Hadley, and she hugged him.

'*Toodle-oo pip-pip, old chap. Tally-ho,*' said Mason in a plummy English accent, handing him the newspaper.

'No one talks like that,' Hal said gruffly, trying to smile. 'Thanks for . . . you know, teaching me the difference between chips and fries.'

'That's essential information,' Mason replied.

Hal jumped as the Comet's horn blared. 'Oh, but, I never did that recording for your voice bank.'

'Next time,' Mason replied.

'I hope there is a next time,' Hal said.

'You'd better go.' Hadley smiled. 'Oh wait! I thought about what you asked me, about how I'd do a kidnap as a magic trick? Well, I'd pull a switcheroo, wouldn't I? I'd get someone to grab Marianne as soon as she came out the door and drag her out of sight. Then Mason, dressed as Marianne, would be waiting in the parking lot for Zola to come out of the Silver Scout. He screams, I'd throw him in the trunk and drive around the corner, then we'd jump out, change clothes and walk away.'

Hal stared at Hadley. 'That would work.'

'That was Marianne who screamed, Hal,' Mason said. 'I know her voice.' He tapped his head. 'I've got her funny accent lodged up here.'

'Like I said before,' Hadley said, 'kidnapping isn't magic.'

'Hal!' shouted Uncle Nat, hanging out the door of the carriage.

'I'd better run.' Hal smiled at his friends, then broke away, sprinting to his uncle and jumping through the doors before they closed. Going to the window, he waved madly at Hadley and Mason, who ran alongside the train as the Comet left the platform. Hal craned his neck to watch them disappear and felt a hand on his shoulder. Uncle Nat gave him a sympathetic look.

'Friendship is the traveller's gift, but farewells are a traveller's curse.'

CHAPTER TWENTY-SEVEN

TELLING TIME

'Come with me,' Uncle Nat said. 'I suspected you might feel blue after Reno, so I've arranged a surprise.'

Hal followed his uncle, but his head was buzzing. He stumbled as they snaked through the train to the sightseer lounge. The morning sun flashed from the windows of cars and shops as the train trundled through the suburbs of Reno.

'Here we are.' Uncle Nat stopped beside a booth occupied by Seymour Hart, his briefcase on the table. Sliding into the seat opposite, Uncle Nat indicated Hal should sit down beside him.

'Is it time?' Seymour smiled and Uncle Nat nodded.

'Time for what?' asked Hal.

'I've bought you a present.' Uncle Nat sounded excited.

Seymour opened his briefcase, took out a black box, and slid it across the table.

Hal looked at his uncle. 'A present?'

'Go on, open it,' Uncle Nat said eagerly. 'Happy birthday!'

Lifting the lid, Hal saw a navy-faced watch with silver

hands and rim. He lifted it out by its chunky rubber strap.

'My finest junior-explorer watch,' Seymour said proudly. 'Three hands for telling the time the old-fashioned way, and if you press that button on the side . . .' Hal did, and the face lit up turquoise, displaying the time digitally. 'It has a compass, calendar, stopwatch, and it's waterproof, down to a hundred feet. It can be worn in the bath, shower or while you're swimming in the sea.'

'Put it on,' Uncle Nat suggested.

Hal unbuckled the strap, slipped the watch on and fastened it, feeling the weight of it on his wrist.

'Every traveller needs a watch,' said Uncle Nat, looking at him nervously. 'Do you like it?'

'I love it!' Hal whispered. 'It's brilliant – it's . . .' He threw his arms around his uncle, hugging him tight, surprised to find he was blinking back tears.

'Oh, I am glad.' Uncle Nat beamed.

Hal sat back, admiring his watch.

'I knew we'd picked a winner,' said Seymour, winking

at Uncle Nat. He closed his briefcase, locked it and patted it.

That case is Seymour's most precious possession, Hal thought, *but he still fell for our switcheroo.* The clues from the kidnap spun about his head: Marianne's yellow dress, pots of pens strewn across the bedroom, the ransom note, the sweet wrapper, the purple hoodie. The answer was in there somewhere. Why couldn't he see it?

Seymour got to his feet. 'W-well, if we've completed our business, I'm going to get myself a celebratory cup of coffee.' His eyes twinkled. 'It's been a pleasure spending *time* with you. Have a good day now.'

'I know that look.' Uncle Nat studied Hal. 'What's going on in that head of yours?'

Hal took out his sketchbook, waiting until the watch salesman was out of earshot. 'Hadley said something on the platform in Reno that's made my head jangle.'

'Go on.'

'She said that if the kidnapping were *her* trick, Marianne would have been grabbed, while Mason – dressed as Marianne – would scream and be thrown in the boot of the car.' Hal blinked. 'Do you remember? When we all went chasing after that car . . . *no one was looking in the other direction.*'

Uncle Nat's eyes grew wide.

'And look . . .' Hal flicked to the sketch he'd done of Marianne in the Durham Museum, and then turned to the sketch of her being kidnapped. 'Do you see?'

Uncle Nat's eyes flicked from one sketch to the other. 'See? See what?'

'The shoes.' Hal pointed. 'At the museum, Marianne had on strappy sandals – but here, she's wearing trainers. I didn't see it before, but it's been staring me in the face all this time.'

'Dear Lord!' Uncle Nat pulled the sketchbook closer, studying the two pictures. 'You're right!'

'I don't know who was thrown into the boot of that car,' Hal said, 'but it wasn't Marianne.'

Uncle Nat and Hal stared at each other.

'What if one kidnapper grabbed Marianne when she came out of the Silver Scout, dragged her round the back of the carriage and covered her mouth, while a *fake* kidnapping was staged in the car park?' Hal said. 'After the police finished their search, the kidnappers could bring Marianne back on to the train – hide in a roomette or compartment and make a clean getaway. That's when Marianne could have dropped the sweet wrapper – in the struggle when they brought her back on board.'

'It could be . . .' Uncle Nat hesitated. 'But what about the teeth? And how could the kidnappers have known Marianne would be wearing a yellow dress?' He shook his head. 'And it doesn't explain how Hadley's purple hoodie turned up in coach.'

'I'm missing something.' Hal flipped through the pages of his sketchbook. 'But I'm getting close. I can feel it.'

'If you're right, then there'd be a number of people involved with the kidnapping – and at least one in August Reza's household. It might be a gang.'

'A gang . . .' Hal's neck prickled.

'We should tell the police,' Uncle Nat said.

'But they said my pictures weren't evidence,' Hal protested. 'We have nothing but theories. We need proof.' He glanced down at his picture of Adalbert Cabbage. Did she have something to do with it? He looked at his uncle. 'We should talk to Vanessa Rodriguez.'

'Why?'

'Zola says she's a police officer.' Hal stood up. 'We can tell her what we've uncovered.'

'I see.' Uncle Nat nodded. 'I'll come with you.'

'Wait. First, can you check to see if Adalbert Cabbage is still sat in coach? She should be halfway back on the right. I saw her this morning at breakfast, but she could have got off at Reno.'

Uncle Nat nodded. 'I'll meet you at Vanessa Rodriguez's roomette.'

Hal hurried through the train, feeling as though the truth were pawing at the door of his brain. His chest tightened as he approached the Morettis' empty compartment. Beyond it was Ryan's bedroom, and he felt a flush of guilt about getting him in trouble with his father. Before he could change his mind, he stepped up to the door and knocked.

There was no answer.

Francine appeared in the doorway of the Morettis' room with an armful of sheets.

'Looking for the Jacksons?' she asked. 'They left in the middle of the night. Got off at Salt Lake City.'

'But Mr Jackson said they were going to San Francisco.' Hal felt the hairs on his arms rise.

'The gentleman had to change his plans. He said his momma was sick. It came on awful sudden.' Francine looked at Hal. 'Did his boy have something of yours?'

'Err, yes,' Hal lied. 'I lent Ryan a . . . book – a *Tintin* book. It's my favourite.'

'He might have left it behind, knowing you'd want it back.' Francine pulled an elastic string from her belt with a loop of keys on it. 'Let's see now. There you are.' She unlocked the door and pushed it open. 'Take a look. The room will be empty to Emeryville now.'

'Thank you, Francine.' Hal's heart was beating fast.

'I hope you get your book back,' she said, shuffling off with the bed linen.

Standing in the compartment, Hal could smell Gene's aftershave. He opened every cupboard and drawer, feeling along every shelf, but found nothing. The shower room was empty too.

His eyes fell on the bin and the white plastic bag inside. Someone had tied it shut: a thoughtful gesture for whoever came to empty it. But Gene Jackson didn't strike Hal as the kind of man who was thoughtful. His nimble fingers pulled the knot apart, and he crouched down emptying the contents on to the floor. As he stared at the rubbish, a sequence of pictures formed in his head, flipping seamlessly from one to the next. Hal saw the whole case come together in his mind's eye, and he knew immediately who'd kidnapped Marianne – and *exactly* how they'd done it.

CHAPTER TWENTY-EIGHT

CABBAGE BAGGAGE

'*Arrrgggghhh!*'
Hal heard the cry and realized with horror it was Uncle Nat. He sprinted down the corridor, stopping outside Vanessa Rodriguez's roomette. Uncle Nat was on his knees with his face pushed into the carpet and his arm twisted behind his back. The woman stood over him, holding his wrist up in a tight grip.

'It's me, Nathaniel Bradshaw, from across the hall!' Uncle Nat pleaded. Vanessa Rodriguez let go of him.

'You shouldn't surprise someone when they're wearing headphones,' she said flatly.

'I didn't mean to startle you.' Uncle Nat rubbed his wrist. 'I knocked, but you couldn't hear me. That's why I opened the door and tapped you on the shoulder.' He got to his feet. 'Oh, hello, Hal.'

'Are you all right?' Hal asked.

'Fine.' Uncle Nat turned to Vanessa Rodriguez. 'Hal was right about you being a police officer, then?'

'What gave me away?' Vanessa snorted out a laugh.

'Are you working on the Marianne Reza kidnapping?' Hal asked.

'No. I'm an officer in the Chicago Police Department. I don't have jurisdiction here.'

'But . . .' Hal faltered. 'Zola said you were watching her.'

'I was asked to keep an eye on her.' Vanessa shrugged. 'That's all. I'm travelling to visit a friend in San Francisco.' She rolled her eyes. 'Just my luck to wander into a crime scene.'

'But . . . you warned me about Adalbert Cabbage.'

'Yeah, cos you were cosying up to her at breakfast. She's dangerous – a career criminal – the kind that takes advantage of good people. She pops up from time to time in Chicago. Has a nasty habit of stealing people's identities and tricking old people out of their life savings.' She shook her head. 'Man, I hate crims that target the olds. She'll steal anything . . . wallets, passports, social security numbers –' she waved her hand – 'anything that she can sell.'

'Well *now* she's guilty of theft and, I think, an

accomplice to kidnapping,' Hal said.

'She's what?' Uncle Nat looked at Hal over his glasses.

'You have proof?' Vanessa asked, sounding unfazed.

'Yes.' Hal pulled the pink lipstick from his pocket. 'This was found in the Silver Scout. It's pink, the shade that Adalbert wears. I'm sure, if you test it, you'll find her DNA.'

'Dropping lipstick isn't illegal,' Vanessa said.

'No – but stealing the hard drive from August Reza's computer is.'

'It's missing?'

'Yes. And she's never been invited into the Silver Scout, so how did her lipstick end up in there? I think the hard drive is hidden in the lining of that big coat she wears.'

Vanessa stared at him. 'So why do you think she's involved in the kidnapping?'

'She asked me about it at breakfast, and I told her I thought the kidnapper was a woman. She said I was wrong, that it must have been a short man, and a woman would never do such a thing.' Hal shook his head. 'Why would she say that when she said she hadn't witnessed the kidnapping? She was trying to make me doubt myself, but I never doubt what I draw.'

'Draw?' Vanessa raised an eyebrow.

'Look, I know it's not normal for children to help solve crimes, but we're going to be in Emeryville in a few hours. Do you want to be the police officer that didn't listen to a kid and let the people involved in the Reza kidnapping get away?'

Vanessa stared hard at Hal, and then one side of her mouth curved up into a crooked smile of respect. 'Do we even know if Adleburt Cabbage is still on this train?'

'She's in coach,' Uncle Nat replied. 'I checked.'

'Then I'll call for back-up.' Vanessa looked out the window. 'Where are we?'

'Approaching Truckee,' Uncle Nat replied, 'about to climb into the Sierra Nevada.'

Vanessa reached over her chair to pick up her phone. Her leather jacket opened and Hal glimpsed a handgun. 'Nathaniel, is it?' she said over Hal's head. 'Do me a favour. Go and sit in the sightseer lounge, beside the door to coach. If the suspect leaves the carriage, I need to know, but don't engage with her. She's dangerous. This train is wall-to-wall civilians, and we don't know if she's armed. I don't want a hostage situation. I'll call this in, then I'll come down and join you. We'll sit tight till we've got support. Understand?'

'Right, of course.' Uncle Nat nodded at her, then at Hal, and left.

Vanessa looked at Hal. 'Go sit in your roomette, kid. You've done good – now leave this to the grown-ups.'

'But—'

'This is not a game. Your mother won't be happy if you get hurt.' She dialled a number on her phone and turned her back to him.

'But I haven't told you about . . .' He held up his sketchbook.

'Hello? This is Rodriguez. Put me through to Sergeant Buckey in Omaha.'

Hal tapped Vanessa's elbow, but she shooed him away with her hand, scowling to let him know their conversation was over.

Hal glared at her but withdrew, going into his roomette and closing the door. She hadn't let him finish. He hadn't told her about the switcheroo, or how the kidnapping had really been done.

Dropping into his chair, he stared out of the window at the deep carpet of pine and fir trees fraying at the foot of the distant mountains. If he sat here and did nothing, and the police arrived with their stomping boots, handcuffs and guns, things could go badly for Marianne. He thought about August Reza. *What would he want me to do?*

Hal laid his sketchbook on the table as the town of Truckee arrived like a movie set rolling into position in front of the window – a parade of colourful wooden shops, houses and a bright red fire station. He heard the *ting ting* of a level-crossing bell as the California Comet pulled to a stop beside the platform.

He knew what he had to do.

CHAPTER TWENTY-NINE

DOPPELGANGER

Hal sprinted along the platform to the Silver Scout. His heart was in his throat as he punched in the door code, crept into the private railcar, and slipped into Marianne's bedroom. The room was tidy. The bed was made, and the pots of pens were lined up on the desk once more. He opened the wardrobe and felt a chill as his eyes settled on a canary-yellow dress hanging among the clothes.

Returning to the corridor once the train was moving, he slid his back along the shiny white wall and peered into the meeting room. It was empty, but he could hear a television. He ran silently to the opposite doorway, snatching a glimpse of the lounge, before flattening himself against the wall. Someone was on the sofa watching a cartoon on a laptop. The canned laughter sounded ominous. A pulse throbbed in his head and his chest felt tight. He drew in a deep breath and stepped into the room.

Sitting with his back to the door was Ryan. He was wearing his red T-shirt and blue jeans, but his head brace was unfastened, and his glasses were on the sofa beside him.

Hal said in a loud, clear voice, 'Marianne?'

Ryan spun around. The cropped hair, the boy's clothes, the headgear and glasses were a good disguise, but she'd answered to her real name.

Marianne's eyes snapped wide at the sight of Hal, and they stared at each other.

'Marianne.' Hal moved towards her.

She lifted her finger to her lips, hushing him soundlessly. She closed the laptop, silencing it, and nodded to the corridor behind Hal. He heard a man singing to himself in the kitchen.

'*Help!*' she mouthed.

There was a clang from the kitchen, an angry exclamation, then the thudding of approaching footsteps. Gene Jackson lumbered in, munching on a sandwich. His eyes bulged when he saw Hal. A lump of what looked like pastrami fell from the corner of his mouth, splatting on the floor.

'Please don't hurt us, Mr Jackson,' Marianne pleaded, unclipping the braces from her face. 'Hal's my friend!'

Gene wiped his mouth, looking from Marianne to Hal.

'It's all right, Mr Jackson,' said Hal calmly. 'I know you didn't kidnap Marianne.' He turned to her. 'You kidnapped yourself.'

Marianne gasped, and Gene started to laugh, choking on his food. His face went purple and he thumped his chest as he coughed and laughed and coughed. Recovering, he pointed at Hal. 'That Limey kid is cleverer than the whole US police force!'

'Shut up.' Marianne scowled at Hal. 'Who've you told?'

'You're going to be in big trouble when people find out what you've done,' said Hal. 'Your mum and dad are so worried. Half the American police is looking for you. Zola's being questioned by the FBI . . .'

'I don't CARE!' Marianne spat. 'It's not my fault the police are stupid. Anyway, serves Zola right. She's a Zircona spy. She thought if she pouted at Dad and fluttered her eyelashes, he'd tell her his secrets.'

'You chose her to witness your kidnapping, didn't you?' Hal said. 'You set her up because you were jealous of the attention she was getting from your dad.'

Marianne narrowed her eyes and shrugged. 'What if I did?'

'Don't you care how upset your parents are?'

'Don't they care how upset *I AM*?' Marianne stomped her foot. 'You wouldn't understand. Look how your uncle dotes on you.' Her nostrils flared and her voice became nasty. 'I'll bet that you live at home with your mom and dad, and every day, after school, they ask you how your day was. I bet you have family meals, and *your* parents *play* with you.'

'Yes, they do,' Hal said, and Marianne's face twisted.

'I'll bet that while you're here in America,' she whispered angrily, 'they miss you.'

Hal felt the ever-present ache of homesickness. He missed his family, and he knew they'd be missing him too. He nodded.

'Yeah, well, my parents *don't*.' Marianne's eyes glistened. 'Do you know how often I see my parents? Once every few months. And since they split up, I see them separately, so even less. They were so intent on saving the world with new technology, and brokering peace for the UN, that they stopped loving each other, and then they stopped loving me.'

'I saw your dad's face after you were kidnapped,' Hal said quietly. 'It was awful. I know he loves you.'

'You don't *know*.' Marianne let out an ugly laugh. 'He has me for a week before I have to go back to France, and how do we spend it? On this stinking train, talking to two-faced journalists like Zola.' She clenched her fists. 'I drew him a whole comic about a train of the future. He hasn't even looked at it.'

'If you talk to him . . .'

'He doesn't listen!' she shouted. 'I told them I didn't want to go to boarding school, but they sent me anyway. I hate France. They said it would be good for me, but it's so far away.' A tear ran down her cheek. 'I wanted to come home, but no – they think I need to *toughen up*.' Her jaw clenched. 'Well, do you think I'm tough enough for them now?' An ugly smile curled her lips. 'They'll listen to me *now*, won't they?'

Gene sat down, chewing on his sandwich. 'This is better than watching a soap opera.'

'They *will* listen –' Hal nodded – 'which is why you can stop this now. It's over.'

'It's over when I say it's over!' Marianne's temper flashed.

'Yeah.' Gene sat up. 'This ain't just about teaching August and Camille a lesson. It's about people getting what's owed to them.'

'You want your ransom money?' Hal asked.

'Damn straight I do,' Gene replied. 'That's my fee for being a part of this risky pantomime. Me and Adie got plans – we're going to Mexico to get married.'

'How did you know we were here?' Marianne asked, her eyes narrowing. 'Did Ryan tell?'

'He didn't want any part of this, did he?' Hal asked Gene. 'But you made him.'

'Kid's a wuss,' Gene grunted. 'Can't believe he's my son.'

'Ryan tried to warn me by writing in my sketchbook,' Hal said. 'But I didn't know what he meant. No, it wasn't him that told me. It was your shoes.'

'My shoes?' Marianne's brow furrowed.

232

'When you were in the museum, you were wearing sandals, but the person thrown into the boot of the car was wearing trainers. Hadley helped me see how the kidnap could be like a magic trick. And in a trick, the person who disappears is always in on it. You had to be in on it too – Gene, Adalbert and Ryan were your accomplices.' He saw from her expression that he was right. 'That's why you snuck into coach wearing a disguise, isn't it? To meet up with them before the kidnap. It wasn't to apologize to me. You made up that story about Seymour Hart following you because we saw you.' Hal glanced from Marianne to Gene. 'I just don't know how you're connected.'

'Gene is my uncle,' Marianne replied, 'or rather, ex-uncle. He was married to my mum's twin sister, but now he lives with Adie. Ryan is my cousin.'

'So *that's* why you look similar.'

'Stuck-up cow threw me out over a few card games, then took me for every cent I had,' Gene said bitterly. 'But I got Adie now. She's the woman of my dreams.'

'This whole thing was your idea, wasn't it?' Hal said to Marianne. 'You chose a bright yellow dress for your kidnap costume because it stood out, and bought two of them – one for you and one for Ryan. At Omaha, once everyone was in the Silver Scout, you sent Woody off to get you a drink, telling Zola to meet you outside because every trick needs an audience. Who better than a respected journalist? You picked up Hadley's purple hoodie on your way out, sprinting away from the Silver Scout to the hedge around the car park. You put the hoodie on, tucking your yellow dress up inside, leaving your black leggings on show. When Zola stepped out, you screamed. I heard you. Mason heard you. It could only have been you. But we *saw* Ryan, in an identical yellow dress and a blonde wig, struggling while Adie dragged him backwards and threw him in the boot. When the car drove away, we all ran after it. In the commotion, you went around the back of the train, where Gene was waiting with Ryan's clothes, the head brace and glasses.'

'Kid's smart,' said Gene, nodding.

'Shut up,' Marianne snapped.

'You put the glasses on,' Hal continued, 'pulled your hood up and hurried down the train to coach. You popped one of your favourite sweets in your mouth, probably to calm yourself, and dropped the wrapper. You almost got caught when you passed Frank Moretti, who recognized the hoodie and mistook you for Hadley. In the restroom, you put on Ryan's clothes, tied your hair back, and strapped on the head brace. You stuffed the hoodie in the bin and went to Gene's compartment, pretending to be Ryan—'

'Wait! That wasn't the plan!' Gene looked at Marianne. 'You were meant to get changed in the compartment!'

'But she'd made a promise to Hadley to return her hoodie,' Hal replied, looking at Marianne. 'And you wanted to keep your promise, didn't you?'

'Her dad made it for her birthday,' she said quietly.

'You idiot!' Gene said angrily. 'You could've ruined everything!'

'I didn't though, did I?' Marianne shot back. 'It's *my* plan, and I'm in charge of what happens.'

Hal saw a mean look flicker across Gene's face.

'In the compartment, Gene cut off your hair,' Hal continued. 'I found it in the bin. That's when I realized you and Ryan had switched places. It explained why Ryan didn't remember writing in my sketchbook. The real Ryan is with Adie, hiding in coach, isn't he?' He thought back to the comic-book rucksack he'd seen on the empty seat beside her. 'It was all going so well, until last night. Through the adjoining wall of the compartments, you overheard our pizza party. You listened as we talked about clues and magic tricks, and you panicked. We were getting close to working it out, so you pretended to leave the train at Salt Lake City and came to hide in here.'

'You weren't that close,' muttered Marianne.

'The one thing I can't figure out is the teeth,' Hal said. 'How did you do that? Have you been pulling your own teeth out?'

Marianne laughed, a high unnerving sound. 'Did you like that?' she asked sarcastically. 'Adie said I should come up with something gruesome, to make the kidnapping seem real.'

'But they've been arriving at Reza Technologies . . . The papers said the DNA proved they were *your* teeth.'

'They *are* my teeth,' Marianne replied. 'They're my baby teeth. I have all of them in my jewellery box.' She leaned forward. 'Didn't you know? The tooth fairy doesn't come to boarding school.' She gave him a cold smile. 'You think you're pretty clever, don't you?'

'We'll see,' Hal said.

'What's that supposed to mean?'

'I know you're angry, Marianne,' Hal said softly, 'but you're hurting people.'

Marianne straightened her shoulders. 'I'm the hurt one.'

'You're not a bad person, Marianne. Otherwise you wouldn't have returned Hadley's hoodie.' Marianne pursed her lips. 'But you've caused a lot of trouble, and you must put things right – take responsibility for it.' Hal gave her a gentle smile. 'At the next station, I think you should come with me, back on to the train, and give yourself up to Vanessa Rodriguez – she's a police officer.'

'She's what?' Gene looked appalled.

'And if I don't?' Marianne lifted her chin.

'That's up to you,' Hal said calmly. 'I haven't told anyone about the kidnapping or that I'm here. I'm counting on you to do the right thing.' He looked her in the eyes and swallowed. 'I'm at your mercy.'

CHAPTER THIRTY

A DOUBLE-
CROSSING

'I'll settle this right now,' Gene said, jumping up and grabbing Hal by the shoulders, 'by throwing the little know-it-all off the train.'

'Uncle Gene, stop!' Marianne grabbed his arm, but he shrugged her off.

'Don't go soft now, princess. You're in as much trouble as I am.'

At the back of the curved lounge was a door which opened out over the tracks. Dragging Hal towards it, Gene kicked at the handle. It swung open and the clattering sound of wheels on metal flooded in.

Marianne cried out. 'This isn't the plan!'

'Neither is turning ourselves in!' shouted Gene.

'I never said we'd hand ourselves in!' Marianne yelled. 'Just let me *think*.'

'I'm done with thinking,' Gene growled. 'Adie said you'd turn chicken and she was right.'

'Don't trust Adie,' Hal cried, struggling to free himself. 'Adie's not even her real name.'

'Shut up,' said Gene, shoving him forward.

Hal grabbed frantically at furniture, gripping the doorframe to stop himself tumbling out. A wave of vertigo turned his legs to jelly. Beside the tracks, the ground dropped away into a deep canyon.

'Adie's a con artist!' he shouted. 'If you don't know her real name, she's conning you too!'

'Adie loves me . . .'

'Does she? Did you know that at Denver station, she stole the hard drive from August Reza's computer?' A look of confusion crossed Gene's face. 'She's planning to sell it. Go upstairs and look if you don't believe me. She's double-crossing you!'

Gene wrenched Hal back into the lounge, throwing him on to the carpet. 'If you're lying, I'm throwing you straight out that door.' And with that, he stomped upstairs to the bedroom.

Hal pressed his face into the floor as Marianne closed the lounge door with a *clunk*.

'I didn't mean for anyone to get hurt,' she said quietly.

'You have to stop, Marianne,' Hal said, sitting up. 'Turn yourself in and this will all be over.'

'I . . . I can't,' she said, her face fearful.

There was an angry shout and a loud crashing noise. Gene thundered back down the stairs. 'She *took it*!' he spat. 'Double-crossing, thieving woman.' He jabbed a finger at Marianne. 'Did you know about this?'

'Of course not.' Marianne scowled. 'Adie's *your* friend. *You* got her involved.'

'Women!' Gene shook his head and rolled up his sleeves. 'You're all sweet smiles, and promises of marriage in Mexico, but when a man's head is turned, you throw him to the hounds. How do I know you weren't planning to let me take the fall this whole time?'

'Because, Uncle Gene, we're family.' Marianne's face was serene. Hal's heart sank as she walked over to the bar and opened a drawer, taking out a small silver pistol. She handed it to him. 'And I'm on *your* side.'

Hal suddenly felt very afraid. 'Marianne, *no*,' he said, his mouth turning dry.

'Take him hostage,' she said coldly, pointing at Hal. 'We can use him as insurance.'

'Smart cookie.' Gene smiled, a look of admiration on his face 'I got just the thing for taking care of insurance.' He put his hand in his pocket and pulled out a pair of handcuffs. As he did, Hal saw a tiny silver key tumble to the carpet.

'What do you have those for?' Marianne frowned.

'Like I said – Adie thought you'd turn chicken,' he replied.

'Mr Jackson?' Hal picked up the key, holding it up. 'You dropped this.'

'Hand it over,' said Gene, waving the handcuffs threateningly.

'Of course.' Hal passed the key from his right hand to his left and put it into Gene's waiting palm. Gene shoved it in his pocket, then clapped a handcuff on Hal's wrist. He dragged him backwards to the staircase, passed the cuffs around the brushed-aluminium banister, and locked the open cuff on to Hal's other wrist. Hal slid down to sit on the bottom stair, with both his arms fastened behind his back.

'Now,' said Gene, turning to Marianne, 'we gotta make sure that ransom money's been paid. I'll call from the payphone when we reach the next station and—'

There was a screech of metal and the Silver Scout juddered, making Gene and Marianne stumble. The California Comet was slowing down on a wide curve of track.

240

'What was that?' Marianne looked about, clearly scared. 'We're nowhere near the next station.'

Sirens blasted. Craning his neck to look through the panoramic window, Hal saw a line of police cars driving down a dirt road that cut across the track, throwing up clouds of yellow dust as they skidded to a stop.

'You lied!' Gene shouted at Hal.

'It's not too late to give yourself up,' Hal said to Marianne, ignoring Gene.

'I've already made my decision,' she replied.

Hal watched a swarm of police officers burst out of the cars, fanning out around the carriage. Gene and Marianne stared out the window.

While they were looking the other way, Hal reached his fingers into his back trouser pocket and pulled out a small silver key.

'Armed police!' a voice called from outside. 'Come out with your hands up!'

'What do we do?' hissed Gene, ducking down.

'We negotiate,' said Marianne. 'Pretend I'm a hostage – take me outside. Demand a car to the airport and make it believable.'

'What about the kid?' Gene flicked his head back to Hal.

'Forget about him,' said Marianne. 'I'm the one they want.'

With the key pinched between his fingers, Hal tried to slot it into the keyhole in the handcuffs, but, unable to see what he was doing, he struggled to find it, and his fingertips were becoming sweaty. *If Houdini did this underwater*, he thought, *I can do it too.*

'OK,' said Gene, getting to his feet. 'You ready?' Not waiting for an answer, he grabbed Marianne around the waist, kicked open the door once more, and shouted, 'I wanna negotiate! I got Marianne Reza right here. Don't you think about trying anything.' He held up the gun. 'I want a car to the airport in ten minutes, or I'll shoot her.'

He pulled Marianne back into the carriage and slammed the door shut, just as Hal felt the key slot into the lock.

'What are you looking at?' Marianne asked Gene, who was staring hard at her, his gun still pointing at her chest.

'Why *pretend* you're my hostage when you can be for real?' Gene leered at her.

'Uncle Gene . . .'

Hal turned the key and, with one hand loose, quickly freed his other, letting the handcuffs fall silently on to the carpet.

'I don't see why I should split the ransom,' Gene continued. 'I'm the one with the gun, and I'm getting sick and tired of being ordered about by a kid.'

Marianne looked frightened, and Gene sneered. 'Not so high and mighty now, are we, Princess? You know, Adie and I weren't *really* going to let you go when we got to Emeryville. We were going to take you to an out-of-the-way lock-up she has and double the ransom. Why settle for ten million when you can have twenty?'

Neither Gene nor Marianne were looking at Hal. He clenched his fists, and before he had time to think, he launched himself at the gun in Gene's hand.

'Hal!' Marianne screamed, as he cannoned into Gene.

'What the—?' Gene exclaimed as the two of them tumbled to the carpet and the gun clattered to the floor.

They rolled and twisted, Hal fighting to escape Gene's grasp. But the man was a wrestler, and pinned Hal easily to the floor.

'That was a big mistake, kid.'

CHAPTER THIRTY-ONE

CONFESSIONS AND COMMOTIONS

Hal stared up into Gene's face in horror. A vision of his mother and father holding little Ellie appeared in his head. Gene grabbed the gun, accidentally pulling the trigger, but . . .

There was no *bang*, just a *click*, and from the end of the barrel a small flame flickered.

Gene gawped at it, his brow furrowed. 'What in the—?' But before he finished, there was an almighty *crunch*, as Marianne smacked a glass lamp stand over Gene's head.

Gene slumped to the floor, groaning, and Hal scrambled out from underneath him. He looked up at Marianne, his heart hammering.

'Are you OK?' she gasped. 'It wasn't a real gun. It's Pop's cigar lighter.' Her breathing was heavy. 'I didn't know how else to make him believe I was on his side when I was really on yours.'

'You tricked him?' Hal thought he might faint.

'I would *never* have given him a real gun!' Marianne looked aghast.

Gene moaned, and Marianne sprang to the back door, throwing it open. 'Help!' she cried, waving at the police officers. 'Come quick! We knocked him out!'

Officers dashed across the tracks, storming into the carriage. Hal and Marianne were brought outside, and blankets were gently wrapped around their shoulders. Moments later, a woozy-looking Gene was dragged, staggering, from the Silver Scout in handcuffs and shoved into the back of a police car.

'It wasn't my idea!' Gene called out. 'I didn't do anything. Marianne Reza kidnapped herself!'

One of the officers spoke into her radio. 'We have the two kidnap victims safe,' she declared. 'Repeat: the kidnap victims are safe.'

'I'm not a victim,' mumbled Marianne to Hal. 'I have to turn myself in.'

Hal squeezed her hand. 'I'll help you explain.'

'Hal!' Uncle Nat dashed towards them, wide-eyed. 'Are you OK?' His uncle swept him into a hug. 'Are you hurt?' He checked Hal, then looked at Marianne. 'Marianne – you're safe? What happened?'

'Uncle Nat, why did the train stop? And all the police officers . . . where did they come from?'

'You *disappeared*,' Uncle Nat said, obviously cross. 'I found your sketchbook in the roomette, with Marianne's hair inside it. I realized what you'd realized and told Vanessa that Gene had kidnapped Marianne.'

'I'm very sorry, Mr Bradshaw,' Marianne said, 'but Uncle Gene didn't kidnap me. I kidnapped myself.'

'I beg your pardon?' Uncle Nat's brow furrowed. '*Uncle Gene?*'

Hal giggled, then so did Marianne, and then Hal found he couldn't stop laughing, and tears fell from his eyes. 'She kidnapped herself!' he repeated, and the two of them shook with peals of laughter.

'I'm not sure that's funny,' Uncle Nat said.

'I'm sorry.' Hal wiped his eyes. 'It's just such a stupid thing to do.' He nudged Marianne. 'You're a total idiot.'

'I know.' She replied and they both laughed again, overcome with relief that it was over.

'But you saved me from Gene,' said Hal, wiping his eyes. 'Thank you.'

'No – you saved me,' said Marianne. 'But how did you get out of those handcuffs?'

'Magic,' Hal whispered, and they both giggled.

There was a commotion a little way off as a sophisticated-looking woman with short blonde hair, in a black dress and high heels, was manhandled off the train by Vanessa Rodriguez.

'Help me, someone!' the blonde woman cried out. 'This woman is hurting me!'

'Stand down!' Vanessa Rodriguez barked at the officers drawing near, holding out her police badge. 'This is Adalbert Cabbage, true name Karen Cunningham, suspected of fraud and extortion on a grand scale. We are taking her in for questioning regarding the Reza case. Someone read her

her rights.' Gone was the red wig and blue coat, but Hal recognized Adie at once. He looked at Gene, whose face was pressed to the window of the police car. His mouth was open in shock as he stared disbelieving at the woman he'd thought was going to marry him in Mexico.

'Who should I confess to?' Marianne whispered to Hal.

'Vanessa,' Hal said, keeping a tight hold of Marianne's hand. 'I'll come with you.'

Vanessa Rodriguez blinked with surprise as they approached her.

'I wish to turn myself in,' Marianne said, a tremor in her voice. 'I am responsible for staging my own kidnapping.'

'Really?' Vanessa stared at her. 'Let me guess, you told Adalbert Cabbage you wanted to kidnap yourself, and she said it was a brilliant idea, encouraged you and helped make your idea into a reality?'

Marianne looked ashamed. 'Yes.'

'Yeah, well, I would arrest you, but you're a minor, a kid. A girl with a crazy idea to kidnap herself. You should probably be grounded for a year or made to pick up litter. That woman's an adult. She knows what's illegal, and she also knows what kinda money she might be able to get her hands on by taking advantage of the dumb kid of a billionaire.'

'Hey!' Marianne scowled. 'I'm not dumb!'

Hal kicked her ankle.

Vanessa looked at Hal. 'You worked all this out?'

Hal nodded, unable to stop a smile from creeping over his face.

'Then I should arrest you too, Mr Beck,' Vanessa said, 'for withholding information.' Hal spluttered, but then her lip curled, and she winked. 'Gotcha!'

'Officer Rodriguez,' Hal said. 'Gene Jackson has a silver key in his pocket. It's for the padlock on my uncle's suitcase. Do you think you could get it back for me, please?'

'Why does he have your uncle's key?'

'One day I'll show you the French Drop and you'll understand,' he replied cryptically.

Vanessa shook her head, walking over to the police car in which Gene was sat, still gawping at Adie.

'Hal!' For a second Hal didn't recognize the boy coming towards him. He looked different without the face brace and glasses, and he was carrying the lizard, Julio, on his arm.

'Ryan! Are you OK?'

Ryan nodded. 'I've been trapped in coach, praying for this whole thing to be over.' He smiled. 'And now it is, thanks to you.'

'I never would have solved it if you hadn't given me that secret message.' Hal nodded at the lizard. 'What's happening to Julio?'

'Adie ditched him.' Ryan rubbed Julio's scaly back, and the lizard rolled his tongue with pleasure. 'He didn't want to be a part of the kidnapping any more than I did. I'm hoping Mom will let me keep him.'

Marianne had hung back, hiding behind Hal. He stepped aside and pulled her forward to face Ryan. She stared at the ground, mumbling an apology, but they all three looked up as they heard the crescendoing *ffdd-ffdd-ffdd* of two helicopters that landed a little way off.

'It's Dad,' Marianne said, her voice full of dread.

Cars were sent to the helicopters, people shouted into radios, wheels spun. Marianne clung tightly to Hal's hand until a police car arrived and August Reza jumped out of the passenger seat.

'Mari? Marianne!'

Marianne smiled awkwardly as her father ran to her, scooping her up and kissing the top of her head. 'You wilful, deceitful, stupid –' he kissed her between each reprimand – 'darling, beautiful girl.'

'*Mon petit chou-fleur!*' A tall woman in a powder-blue suit got out of the back of the police car and hurried over to join them. 'Mari!' she cried. 'Your hair!'

'*Je suis désolée, Maman.*' Marianne was crying now, and her father set her down so her mother could hug her.

'You are the artful little fox, no? Making the monkey out of all of us.'

'I'm really sorry.' Marianne descended into sobs.

'And Ryan, *est-ce que ça va?*' She reached out with her free arm and took his hand, pulling him close. 'Your mother, she has been very worried. We will take you home with us.'

'Thank you, Auntie Camille.' Ryan nodded. 'Can I bring Julio?' He lifted his arm so she could see the enormous lizard, and she laughed with surprise.

'If you wish.'

249

'Is my hair terrible, Maman?' Marianne said, wanting her mother's attention back.

Camille put a hand to her daughter's cheek. '*Mais non – c'est très chic.*'

'Harrison –' August Reza smiled at him – 'I hear we have much to thank you for. If there's anything we can do to repay you . . .'

'Actually . . . there is one thing,' Hal said. 'But it's not for me. Marianne would like to go to school here, in America, to be close to you. I know it's not my business, but I'd be really pleased if she got her wish.'

Camille and August exchanged a guilty look.

'Oh,' Hal continued, 'and you should take a look at her design for the Reza's Rocket competition. I know she can't enter – it probably isn't allowed because she's your daughter – but you don't want to miss out on a good idea, and she has lots of them. She came to my rescue and saved me from Gene. I owe her.'

Marianne blushed and smiled gratefully at him.

The Rezas and Ryan said their goodbyes and climbed into a car to be driven back to the helicopter. Gene and Adie were gone, taken to jail, and the hubbub died down.

Hal sat down next to Uncle Nat on a rock by the track. 'For the rest of the journey,' Hal said, 'I'm going to sit in the sightseer lounge and only sketch scenery. I promise.'

'Good.' Uncle Nat handed him a cold can of soda. 'I don't think my heart could take any more excitement.'

'Excuse me!' a voice called out. 'Are you Mr Beck and Mr Bradshaw?' A woman in blue Amtrak overalls with a yellow scarf tied around her Afro walked over.

'Yes, we are,' Uncle Nat answered. 'How may we help you?'

'I'm Lori Shelton.' She shook their hands. 'This is Rico, my deputy.' She nodded at a skinny man with a beard who stood behind her chewing gum. 'I'm the driver of the California Comet. A little billionaire bird told me you like your locomotives.'

'Oh, yes.' Hal beamed.

'It's three hours to Emeryville. In my opinion, there's no finer view than the one from up front.' Lori smiled. 'How would you like to finish your journey with us in the driver's cab?'

Hal and Uncle Nat exchanged delighted glances as they followed Lori and Rico to the front of the train.

'Mr Bradshaw!' Francine called out as they passed. 'Time to get back on board.'

'It's all right, Francine,' Uncle Nat replied gleefully. 'We've seats up front.'

The dark-blue-and-silver locomotive was dusty and streaked from its journey across America. Hal could barely contain his excitement as he grabbed on to the ladder, climbing up into the cab, which was the size of the Morettis' bedroom. Two big letterbox windscreens gave them a view of the track ahead. Below them was a wide console covered in buttons, levers and a small, black joystick.

'Welcome,' Lori said. 'Harrison, you take Rico's chair – and press that button, will you?'

251

The famous five-chime horn echoed through the mountain pass, sending a flock of birds shooting into the sky. Hal grinned over his shoulder at Uncle Nat who was sat beside Rico,

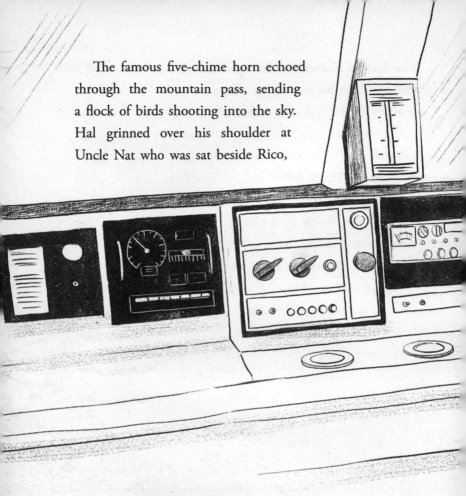

beaming. Lori pushed the throttle, and the engine roared as it heaved the carriages into motion. They rode the rails out of the mountains, picking up speed on the flat, passing through Sacramento, and crossing Davis.

Hal sighed happily as they rattled on to the Benicia–Martinez Bridge, enjoying the *thu-thunk* of the wheels on the tracks as he gazed out over the sparkling water: the twin estuaries of the San Joaquin and Sacramento Rivers draining

into the San Francisco Bay. All was well.
Marianne was back with her parents, and
he was at the helm of the California Comet,
with silver superliners snaking along behind
him.

CHAPTER THIRTY-TWO

THE SILVER SOLARIUM

Watching the thick steel cables wind around the enormous wheels, Hal marvelled that such a simple mechanism could heave trams up and down the hills of San Francisco. It was his last day in America, the sun was shining, and Uncle Nat had promised to show him the sights. Their first stop was the Cable Car Museum.

On the way there, Hal had seen a line of roller-skating nuns zipping past a shop that sold pirate costumes. Crewe was quiet by comparison, but he was looking forward to going home.

'We never wrote our postcards,' he said to his uncle.

'There's still time – and speaking of time . . .' Uncle Nat checked his watch. 'I said we'd meet someone here.'

'And have you ever known me to be late?' a familiar voice asked.

'Zola!' Hal spun around. As always, she was the definition of style, dressed in a mustard blouse, chunky gold necklace and black trousers, her hair natural.

'You didn't think I was going to let you escape the country without giving me the exclusive, did you?' She smiled.

'Exclusive?'

'*Harrison Beck, the Railway Detective*,' she framed the headline with her hands. '*Solves the Kidnap on the California Comet*.' She arched an eyebrow. 'Sound good?'

'Did the FBI let you go?' Hal asked.

'Let me go? They couldn't wait to get rid of me!' She laughed. 'Now, I'm buying you boys lunch. You've a *lot* of explaining to do.'

Zola led them to a restaurant on a hill around the corner. The waiters greeted her like an old friend, and she spoke to them in Italian. The manager took them to a quiet table at the back. As they sat down, Zola pulled out a tiny microphone, plugging it into her smartphone.

'What's that for?' asked Uncle Nat.

'I wasn't joking about the exclusive,' Zola said. 'I want to know everything. But first, I've got a present for Hal.' Reaching into her bag, she brought out a rectangular box wrapped in brown paper. 'This is a congratulations for solving the case.'

Tearing off the paper, Hal found he was holding a model of the California Comet's vintage observation car. The name plate on the side read *Silver Solarium*. 'Oh, it's perfect,' he whispered, marvelling at the detail of the model replica. 'Thank you.'

'The inside lights up,' Zola said, looking pleased by his reaction.

'That's smart.' Uncle Nat held out his hand. 'Can I look?'

'I've got something for you too,' Hal said, pulling Zola's Zircona watch out of his pocket. 'I thought you'd want it back.'

Thanking him, Zola put it back on her wrist. She caught a waitress's attention, and they ordered drinks. 'I told August I was working for Zircona before we boarded the train,' she said. 'He told me he plans to make the design for his batteries public property, to accelerate the use of clean energy. Zircona will use them in their cars, which is great news.' She flipped open her notepad. 'I've so many questions.' Her eyes scanned down the page. 'When did you first suspect something strange was happening?'

'I had a hunch before we even got on the train.' Hal pulled out his sketchbook and opened it to the first drawing from Union Station in Chicago. 'Look. There's Marianne. She's winking. At first, I thought she was winking at Ryan, but she's actually winking at Gene. I sensed at the time something was going on but I didn't know what.'

'How did you work out that Marianne and Ryan had switched?'

'We ate lunch with Ryan and Gene on the first day. Ryan mimed a message to me and scored the word 'help' into my sketchbook.' He showed the page to Zola. 'I thought he was telling me to *help Marianne Reza*, but he wasn't. He wanted me to help him. The message was *Help! Marianne Reza* . . . He might have gone on to say more, but Gene pulled him away. After the kidnap, I kept trying to ask Ryan about it, but he didn't know what I was talking about.'

'Because you were talking to Marianne dressed as Ryan?' Zola asked.

'Exactly. It was only when I found the sweet wrapper that I suspected Marianne was still on the train. Hadley's hoodie turning up confirmed it.'

Their food arrived and Hal paused to eat a few delicious mouthfuls of carbonara.

'Hadley gave me the idea that the kidnap might have been staged, because she's a magician. Then I noticed in my sketches that the shoes that Marianne had been wearing in the museum were not the shoes of the person who was thrown into the boot of the car. But I didn't *definitely* know she was hiding in plain sight, disguised as Ryan, until I found her hair in Gene's bin.

'When Francine said Gene and Ryan had got off the train at Salt Lake City, I realized they must have overheard Uncle Nat and I talking with the Morettis about the case. Worried that we'd work out that Marianne was Ryan, they went and hid in the Silver Scout for the last bit of the journey, but they didn't know that I'd worked out the code for the door.' Hal smiled.

As they ate, he told Zola about the detective work he and the Morettis had done and she pressed him with more questions. 'And Adalbert Cabbage, or Karen Cunningham, if we want to use her real name, has five previous convictions for fraud and extortion. When did you first suspect—?'

'I'm sorry, Zola,' Uncle Nat interrupted, glancing at his watch. 'It's three o'clock. Time's up.'

As his uncle called for the bill, Hal spied three familiar

heads bobbing past the window. He jumped to his feet, his chair scraping backwards, as the restaurant door flew open and Hadley and Mason rushed in. Frank Moretti was a couple of steps behind them, wearing a colourful shirt, his bald patch shining in the afternoon sun.

'I knew you'd do it!' Hadley exclaimed breathlessly.

'Sherlock da Vinci strikes again!' Mason said, picking up Hal and spinning him around.

'Ooh, I like that,' Zola said, making a note. '*Sherlock da Vinci.*'

'Put me down!' Hal laughed. 'What are you doing here?'

'Are you kidding me?' Mason grinned. 'We saw on the news that some dorky English kid had solved the mysterious kidnap of Marianne Reza . . .'

'They wouldn't let me sit down until I called your uncle,' Frank Moretti finished.

'I thought it would be a nice surprise.' Uncle Nat smiled.

'I'm paying the check,' Zola said, waving away Uncle Nat's objections. 'You all go and have fun.'

'Let's go to Pier 39,' Hadley said, pulling Hal towards the door. 'There are rides there.'

'Or the aquarium?' Mason suggested.

'I don't care where we go as long as we can take a cable car,' said Hal. 'Hey, Hadley, you've got something . . .' He reached behind her ear and pulled out a coin.

'You've been practising!' She was delighted.

Hal nodded. 'You'd be proud of me. I used the French Drop to trick Gene and switch a handcuff key for Uncle Nat's suitcase key, which I had in my pocket.'

'You were *handcuffed*?' Mason gawped. 'Tell me everything. Wait! Wait!' He pulled a silver recorder from his pocket. 'Now, tell us – and afterwards, can you say the alphabet?'

Laughing and joking as they went, Hal, Uncle Nat and the Morettis climbed aboard a cable car and headed down to the wharf, where they played in the arcade, ran through a flock of seagulls, and ate ice cream gazing across the bay at the Golden Gate Bridge.

It was a wonderful adventure, the normal kind you have on a day out with good friends.

A NOTE FROM
THE AUTHORS

Dear Reader

We have tried to be as faithful as possible in representing the glorious railways of the United States. But as always, we have taken one or two small liberties with reality for the sake of a good story. We hope you will forgive our indulgences.

The Real California Comet

The California Comet is based very closely on a real railway journey that you can take across America, called the California Zephyr. It's one of the most famous railway journeys in the United States. Like the Comet, it starts at Union Station in Chicago, and over three days and two nights it takes you to Emeryville, just outside San Francisco. It's formed of superliner carriages – like the Comet – and though its timetable is slightly different, it follows an identical route.

The Silver Scout

Throughout the twentieth century, carriages with viewing domes were common on American passenger trains with scenic routes. As Uncle Nat mentions in Chapter Two, six silver dome cars were made especially for the California Zephyr in the 1940s. Many of their names began with the word 'Silver'. There is a real carriage called the Silver Scout, but it is not a dome car. Our Silver Scout is fictional, and based very closely on a real carriage called the Silver Solarium. Like the Scout, the Solarium is privately owned and has been refurbished. At the time of writing, it was available for private charter.

The shining silver appearance of dome cars was part of a global design trend called *Streamline Moderne* – defined by curved edges and aerodynamic lines. This design was so popular that things that couldn't move were made to look aerodynamic – like buildings, vacuum cleaners, and even toasters!

Private Railcars

It really is possible to buy your own private rail carriage and travel around in it, just as August Reza does. In the past, a great many wealthy people had their own private carriages built to their specifications. Today that almost never happens – the very rich prefer private jets. But when a railway company's old carriages go out of service, they are sometimes sold off to save them going to the scrapheap. Usually they need a lot of money spent on them to make them serviceable again. Some people take great pride in restoring vintage carriages to their former glory. These vintage carriages are sometimes called 'varnish'. In America, Amtrak will tow your private car behind most of its trains for a few dollars a mile.

High-Speed Trains

Railways were the backbone of young America, being the dominant mode of travel until the mid-twentieth century. But as cars and planes became more popular, the country's passenger rail system began to decline. If you're travelling today, it's currently faster and cheaper to drive or fly (though we would argue, a lot less fun!).

There are some plans afoot to build new high-speed railway lines in the United States, making trains more appealing for intercity travel. But none on the scale of August Reza's global transport revolution. The Northeast Corridor, where Reza plans his first line, is actually home to the fastest train in America already – Amtrak's very popular Acela service, which can reach speeds of up to 150 mph. But sadly this is only possible on part of the route, meaning that overall the journey is slower than many dedicated high-speed systems in Europe, like France's TGVs, and Germany's ICEs.

Find out more . . .

There are a number of brilliant railway museums in the United States – including the Durham Museum in Omaha, featured in this book. If you're in the UK and would like to learn more about trains, we recommend a visit to the National Railway

Museum in York, which has real-life trains from all over the world. It's where Maya first fell in love with trains.

You can also visit our website to find lots of great resources and learn more about Hal's adventures – find it at **adventuresontrains.com**

Turn the page for an exclusive peek
at Hal's next adventure,

MURDER ON THE SAFARI STAR!

THE SAFARI STATION

Hal licked the edge of his thumb and smudged the lines of charcoal in his sketchbook, teasing them out to look like sharp black quills. The subject of his drawing was nibbling tree bark and glowering at him. The porcupine had a wide, spongey nose, a salt-and-pepper mohawk, long prickly spines, and a tail the length of its body. Hal leaned forward to study its face and the spiky creature huffed, ambling off towards the train shed and flopping into a dusty hole.

'A prickly customer,' Uncle Nat chuckled. His face was shaded from the sun by a broad-brimmed panama hat and he looked every bit the explorer in his crisp white shirt and ivory linen suit.

Hal and Uncle Nat were sat at a table on the veranda outside the departure lounge in Pretoria's Central Garden Station. It was a private rail terminal and the grand country house had grounds like a wildlife park.

'Perhaps you should draw a bird.' Uncle Nat looked pointedly at the prattle of scarlet and grey parrots gossiping with one another in the trees.

Fleetingly, Hal thought of everyone back home in Crewe

having a cold, grey, February half-term holiday. He grinned at the red-and-brown speckled Nguni cattle who were grazing on the other side of the tracks in the morning sunshine.

They had landed at Pretoria airport the previous night and though their hotel was nice, Hal had been itching to see the train they would be travelling on. As soon as they'd woken, he'd begged Uncle Nat to have breakfast at the Central Garden Station, despite the Safari Star not departing until after lunch. He'd read about the train sheds where you could watch mechanics restoring vintage rolling stock. There was a museum as well as the famous animal residents, and he couldn't wait to see them.

As they'd stepped out of the taxi in front of the grand red-brick building with white arches, a porter had greeted them. Their luggage was unloaded beside a glossy bottle-green sign that read *Ackerman Railway* in gold letters. The porter had directed them to the veranda, serving breakfast beside the railway tracks, assuring them she'd take care of their cases.

Hal was so excited, he felt like an army of frogs was bouncing about in his belly. He wasn't sure he'd be able to eat, but managed to consume the fruit and buns with enthusiasm.

Striding towards their table smiling like a hungry crocodile, was a tanned man, with closely-cropped silver hair and beard, dressed in a pink shirt and chalk-white trousers.

'Nathaniel Bradshaw, it's an honour to meet you. I'm Luther Ackerman. Welcome to Central Gardens.' He shook Uncle Nat's hand enthusiastically. 'We're delighted that you're travelling with us. How was your journey here, good? Do the porters have your cases? Yes? You're taking a trip on the Safari Star to Victoria Falls? The Safari Star is the jewel in the Ackerman Railway luxury locomotive fleet.' He looked at Hal. 'And who is your travelling companion?'

'Pleased to make your acquaintance, Mr Ackerman,' Uncle Nat replied, blinking at the barrage of questions. 'This is my nephew, Harrison Beck.'

Hal nodded, keeping his hands behind his back in case the excited man tried to shake them.

'Harrison Beck!' Ackerman leaned back, taking in Hal. 'The railway detective that I've read about in the papers? What an honour. Perhaps you'd like us to rustle up a crime for you to solve whilst you're on the train?' He laughed loudly. 'A theft, perhaps, or a gruesome murder?'

'No thank you, Sir,' Hal replied. 'I'd rather just see the animals.'

'I've been trying to get your uncle on one of my trains for years,' said Ackerman. 'A good review from him will bring a flood of guests.' He leaned down and whispered loudly behind his hand. 'Put in a good word for me.' He laughed again and Hal smiled awkwardly, glancing at his uncle.

'We'd like to visit your workshop, Mr Ackerman,' Uncle Nat said. 'Is it open yet? We're keen to see the locomotives.'

'Call me Luther.' Mr Ackerman clapped Uncle Nat on the back, making his horn-rimmed glasses jump. 'Everything is open for guests of the Safari Star.' He pointed across the track. 'Over there are the engine sheds where we restore the locomotives and fit out the carriages. Beyond is the marshalling yard. Along that path is the original signal box and water tower.' He paused as an ostrich strutted past the fountain beside the veranda. 'Our station is a monument to the golden era of Africa's railways. Explore it to your heart's content.'

'Is it normal to have animals at a station in South Africa?' Hal asked.

'The animals moved in when the station was abandoned in the 1940s,' Luther explained. 'They'd already made this place their home when I bought it, so I didn't have the heart to move them on.'

'It's brilliant,' Hal said.

'I've bothered you for long enough.' Ackerman snapped his heels together and bowed. 'Make yourselves at home. I'll be on the train too, and am at your service, day or night.'

Hal and Nat crossed an iron bridge over the tracks and followed a winding path through the trees towards the sheds. A beetle the size of a chestnut flew clumsily in front of them, crashing into a tree trunk and falling to the ground, spinning on its back, all six of its legs waggling. Uncle Nat pointed ahead of them - sitting on siding tracks were two giant sheds, with a royal blue locomotive visible through their open doors.

They put on hard hats and yellow hi-vis vests as they entered, climbing the stairs to the gallery overlooking the workshop. The sheds echoed with hammer clangs, the whirr of machinery, and the call and response of workers' voices.

'This is amazing,' Hal shouted, gazing down at a view of old carriages and locomotives in various states of repair. A scatter of sparks gushed from a trough beneath the rails and he saw a woman tinkering with the belly of a half-dismantled class 6 loco. She wore green overalls and her arms were streaked with grease. She reminded Hal of his best friend Lenny, who he'd met on board The Highland Falcon. He leaned his sketchbook on the rail to draw her standing underneath the loco. As he smudged black lines to shade in the gleaming metal of the engine boiler, Hal was surprised to see Uncle Nat wander into view.

The mechanic came up from her trough, wiping her arms on an old rag. She had short hair and a snub nose that made her look like an extremely tough pixie. She shook Uncle Nat's hand and he pointed up to Hal.

Hal waved, then followed the gallery along to a set of stairs that led to down the workshop floor.

'Hal,' Uncle Nat strode towards him with a wide smile, 'come and meet Flo, Mr Ackerman's sister. She's the chief engineer here.'

'Hi Hal.' Flo smiled, her eyes dancing playfully, and Hal was struck by how different she was to her brother. 'I was telling your uncle about the Safari Star. She's a fine steam engine. Although there are no longer enough coal and water stops to get her all the way to Victoria Falls, so we switch to a diesel-electric halfway.'

'Are you the driver?' Hal asked.

'No, Sheila and Greg are the steam crew, but I'm coming to oversee the switchover and perform safety checks. If you want to see the Safari Star up close, come to the footplate before we leave.'

'Thanks, I will.' Hal beamed.

'A journey with two different locos is a treat,' Uncle Nat said to Hal. 'The change-over will be fun.' He smiled at Flo. 'Thank you for talking to us. We'll let you get back to your work.'

'See you at the footplate,' Hal said, as he and his uncle walked away, disposing of their hats and vests at the door.

'I'd like to get my hands on a newspaper and have another cup of coffee,' said Uncle Nat as they walked back down the path.

'I want to draw the station from this side of the tracks.' Hal pointed at an iron bench nestled amongst the trees and looked questioningly at his uncle. 'That's a good spot.'

'Sure.' Uncle Nat nodded. 'Come and find me when you're done.'

Sitting down, Hal opened his sketchbook to a clean double page and let his charcoal skim lightly across the paper, capturing the strong horizontal lines of the platform and then marking the vertical lines of the station building.

Hal's focus was broken when something heavy dropped into his lap. He yelled at the sight of an animal the size of a small cat, with course sandy hair, stubby legs and a bushy tail, staring at him with piercing amber eyes.

'Chipo?' A boy's voice called out. 'Chipo, where are you?'

The animal wheeled around, leaping off Hal's lap as a short boy wearing glasses wider than his face, emerged from the trees. He had brown skin, short dark hair, and was wearing a faded yellow T-shirt and combat trousers. 'There you are Chipo!' The animal ran up the boy's arm, coming to sit across the back of his shoulders. 'Sorry,' he said to Hal, 'she thinks you have food.'

'Oh!' Hal pulled a half-eaten bag of peanuts from his pocket. 'They're from the aeroplane.'

Looking at the boy to make sure it was okay, Hal poured three nuts into his palm, and Chipo jumped back onto the bench, grabbing a nut in each paw and stuffing them in her mouth.

'You've made a friend.' The boy laughed.

'What kind of animal is she?' Hal stared at Chipo as she gnawed at the nuts.

'A yellow mongoose.'

'She's cool –' he looked up – 'I'm Hal by the way.'

'I'm Winston.' Chipo grabbed the last nut from Hal and jumped back onto Winston's shoulders. 'Where are you from?'

'England,' said Hal. 'I'm travelling with my uncle on the Safari Star.'

'Were you drawing?' Winston nodded at Hal's sketchpad.

'Yeah, I draw trains mostly.' Hal showed his sketch from the sheds. 'Although on this trip I'm going to draw animals too.' He flipped to the page with the moody porcupine.

Winston laughed. 'It needs a face!'

'It didn't want to sit still.'

'Chipo will sit still if you give her more nuts.'

As if she'd heard and disagreed, Chipo leapt off Winston's shoulder and scampered into the trees.

'Chipo!' Winston called, exasperated. 'Come back here!' He hurried after her and Hal followed. 'Mum said I could bring Chipo on the train if I kept her under control and away from the passengers,' Winston explained. 'Chipo's my best friend, but mongooses usually live in packs and she thinks she's the leader of ours.'

Hal smiled at the news that Winston and Chipo would be on the train. 'Is your mum a passenger?'

'She's the safari guide.' Winston peered through the bushes. 'She knows everything there is to know about animals in South Africa and Zimbabwe. She's a zoologist. This is the first time I've been allowed to come on the train. I've promised to be helpful - you know, run errands, stuff like that - but I really want to see Victoria Falls. Mum made me bring my schoolwork with me.' Winston pulled a face.

'Look, there she is,' Hal pointed.

Chipo was up on her hind legs, sniffing the air. Her ears went flat and she darted across the ground, leaping and catching a damselfly between her paws, which she stuffed in her mouth.

'Oh no! There's Mr Ackerman,' Winston hissed. 'Mum asked me to stay out of his way.' Winston grabbed Chipo, hugging her to his chest. 'C'mon, let's go.'

Intending to follow, Hal glanced over his shoulder and froze. Mr Ackerman was speaking in hushed tones to a short sallow man in a khaki shirt and trousers. His shoulders were hunched, his head low and secretive. The other man nodded, passing Mr Ackerman a roll of money held together by a silver clip – then they shook hands. Goosebumps rose all over Hal's body as he crept backwards, knowing with a chilling certainty that he was witnessing something he shouldn't be, and he didn't want to get caught.

ACKNOWLEDGEMENTS

M. G. Leonard

The most important research for this book was taking the trip from Chicago to San Francisco on the California Zephyr which sadly, I was unable to do. Luckily Sam Sedgman and Tom Leaper did it, and I'm grateful because the book is that much richer for their journey and documenting of that experience.

I would also like to acknowledge Penn and Teller's genius in Hadley's magic tricks. I watched a series of Masterclasses they gave on the basics of magic to create her illusions. It was they who taught me the French Drop, which is now my party trick.

As with each of our Adventures on Trains, I owe a debt of gratitude to Sam for being an excellent co-author. As we craft each book our relationship grows and he has become much more than a colleague and friend. I'm writing this in the middle of the coronavirus lockdown and it has taught me how much I miss seeing him. The past twelve months have been a tumultuous time for me but working with Sam has been a delight. His advice, his insight and support, have buoyed me up, keeping me afloat at difficult times. It is impossible to express how much of my sanity and ability to create I owe to him. The words 'thank you' seem too humble, but they are all I have.

I want to thank everyone at our publishers, Macmillan, for giving our Adventures on Trains series the most incredible launch into the world. They have worked hard to get these stories into the hands and imaginations of readers. In particular I want to cheer the astonishing talents of our editor Lucy Pearse, the brilliant Kat McKenna, Jo Hardacre and Alyx Price.

I'm grateful every day that Kirsty McLachlan, my incredible agent, goes into battle by my side, running into the fray like a berserker, pistols out, drawing fire. I'm lucky to have her for my partner-in-crime. Don't ever leave me, Kirsty.

I'd also like to personally thank every bookseller, librarian and reader who has recommended, read or reviewed our books. I write for you, and your encouragement is oxygen.

I'd like to thank the members of my unconventional family (you know who you are) for inspiring and supporting me, for championing my books and cheering me on.

And Arthur, Seb and Sam – everything is for you, and without you, there'd be nothing. I love you.

Sam Sedgman
Writing can be a lonely struggle sometimes, so I'm glad I was lucky enough to write this book with my friend. Thank you, Maya, for putting up with all my nonsense. You make writing a book look so easy. Working with you continues to be a privilege and a delight and I can't wait for our next adventure together.

This book would not have been possible without Tom Leaper. Tom is my tireless confidant, game travel companion, and brilliant partner. You are always so full of love and support and know how to make me feel better when I doubt myself. Thank you, always.

I dragged Tom from Chicago to San Francisco on board the real-life California Zephyr as research for this book – an experience I will treasure forever. Thank you to the Zephyr's train crew for the boundless warmth and enthusiasm that filled our journey with joy and inspiration.

Thank you to my parents, who gave me all the tools I needed to become a writer, and plenty more besides. Thank you especially for all our adventures together as a family to incredible places around the world, which have shaped Hal's wonder at the joys of travel.

I continue to be dazzled by my work family – my incredible agent Kirsty McLachlan, and the wonderful team at Macmillan who make the trains run on time. Thanks to Lucy Pearse, our editor – you are always so calm and clear-headed. To Kat and Jo and Alyx and Sam and everyone else who has worked so hard for us. You're all brilliant.

Hal's drawings are brought to life by our magnificent illustrator Elisa Paganelli, who works so quickly and so accurately and somehow manages to see right inside our heads. You're alarmingly talented. Thank you.

Thanks too to Sam Sparling, who always asks if I want to stay for dinner.

A book is nothing without the booksellers and librarians who share it with readers. My enormous thanks to all of you who did such a magnificent job getting *The Highland Falcon Thief* into the hands of readers everywhere. Thank you for being nice about our book when there are so many to choose from. And the biggest thanks of all to our readers, whose enthusiasm means so much. This book is for you. I hope you liked it.

M. G. Leonard is the internationally bestselling author of the Battle of the Beetles trilogy and the non-fiction companion, *The Beetle Collector's Handbook. Beetle Boy* won the Branford Boase award and has been translated into 37 languages worldwide. She and her friend, Sam Sedgman, created the bestselling Adventures on Trains series after meeting and working together at the National Theatre. She is a beetle expert and lives in Brighton with her husband and two sons.

Sam Sedgman is a bestselling novelist, playwright and award-winning digital producer. His work has been performed internationally and shortlisted for the Courtyard Theatre award. Written with his friend, M. G. Leonard, *The Highland Falcon Thief* was Sam's first book for children. A lifelong mystery enthusiast, he grew up with a railway at the bottom of his garden and has been mad about trains ever since. He lives in London.

Elisa Paganelli was born in Italy and since childhood, hasn't been able to resist the smell of paper and pencils. She graduated from the European Institute of Design in Turin and worked in advertising, as well as running an award-winning design shop and studio. She now collaborates as a freelance designer with publishers and advertising agencies all over the world, including designing and illustrating *The House With Chicken Legs* (Usborne) and the Travels of Ermine series (Usborne).